D1605751

Home Run

By
Bernadette Marie

This is a fictional work. The names, characters, incidents, places, and locations are solely the concepts and products of the author's imagination or are used to create a fictitious story and should not be construed as real.

5 PRINCE PUBLISHING AND BOOKS, LLC
PO Box 16507
Denver, CO 80216
www.5PrinceBooks.com

ISBN 13: 978-1-63112-008-4 ISBN 10: 1631120085
Home Run
Bernadette Marie
Copyright Bernadette Marie 2014
Published by 5 Prince Publishing

Front Cover Viola Estrella
Author Photo: Damon Kappel 2009

First Edition/First Printing February 2014 Printed U.S.A.

5 PRINCE PUBLISHING AND BOOKS, LLC.

To Stan,
Together we have made a home run with our little team

Acknowledgements

To my husband:
For the days no laundry is done or the dishes pile
up…for the times when the emotions of the characters
trump my own…thank you. Your belief in me to let me live
this dream…well you know…You're my everything!

To my private hockey team:
You boys make me so proud. I love our little family.
You give me lots of inspiration to do what I do!

To my mom, dad, and sister:
Thanks for giving me a foundation to build this family
in which readers have fallen in love with.

To Connie and Sara:
Could I have pushed the limits any harder? You've
made this possible! You've helped me achieve it!

To Audrey:
Remember, I am not responsible for your addiction!
But I'm sure glad it became one!

Dear Reader,

I am very excited to bring you the seventh book in the Keller Family series.

We have followed Christian Keller since he was a young boy learning to deal with his mother's illness and his parents' separation. But he's all grown up now.

Victoria Lincoln, whom we met in book 5, has captured Christian's heart. But tragedy threatens to separate them forever.

One of the things I hear most from readers is how they love the compassion of the Keller men and the strength of the women. It has been the force in my writing so many stories for this amazing family.

I hope you will enjoy Christian and Victoria's compelling story as much as the others.

Be sure to keep reading as you will find the first chapter of book eight *The Acceptance*, when we get to know Tyler Benson, the eldest son of Regan and Zach Benson—the couple that started it all.

Happy Reading,

Bernadette Marie

Home Run

Chapter One

There was a pure energy in the car as they drove away from the arena. Christian Keller had it all, just when he thought he'd lost it.

His career-ending injuries were just the start to finding out he could keep going and that's what he was doing.

He'd just watched his sister perform with her husband, on stage at the Bridgestone Arena right there in Nashville. Hometown kids making it big time.

As his best friend Dave pulled out of the parking lot the number one country song came on the radio, and wouldn't you know it, it was Clara and Warner Wright, his sister and her husband.

Christian's fiancée, Victoria, hugged his arm and slid across the back seat as close as she could to him. "That was the best concert ever. Your sister and Warner were phenomenal. *The Broke Tourists* are one of my favorite bands. And that Savannah and her hair!"

Ashley, Victoria's sister, turned in her seat and looked at her. "I know, right? Do you think we could buy hair like that?"

They both laughed, but Christian just took in the ambiance.

His career as a baseball player was over. He had come to grips with that. It had caused him a lot of emotional and physical pain over the past year, but now he had new things to look forward to.

They were already talking about him coming into the organization as management. The woman of his dreams had accepted his marriage proposal and wore his ring. And tonight, he'd take her home to the home he had built—for them. It was a surprise and he had something very special planned.

"You know," Victoria continued. "Ali would love a Savannah wig. We should think about marketing them."

"My kids and their tastes," Ashley added.

Laughter filled the car and then a scream pierced the air.

A blinding white light forced him to cover his eyes.

Christian sat up in bed. His heart was racing. His face and hair were wet. And he was alone.

He threw his head back against his pillow.

Of course he was alone. He'd been alone for almost a year and the replay of that night wouldn't give him any peace.

Christian rolled to his side and he looked at his phone on the night stand. It was five-thirty in the morning. He let out a grunt and rolled out of bed.

It took a minute for his knee to be stable under him. His shoulder ached, as it had since the surgery after the accident.

He flipped on the light in the bathroom and looked at himself in the mirror. The jagged scar on his forehead was beginning to fade, but it would always remind him that on that night he'd lost everything. His career. His best friend. And even if her life wasn't taken—he'd lost his fiancée.

Well that was life now. She had a lot to deal with too.

Christian splashed his face with cold water.

Victoria's life had changed drastically when that drunk driver crossed the median. She'd lost her sister in that moment. Her leg was shattered. And she was the next of kin to her niece and nephew, whom she was now raising.

A single woman trying to advance her career and plan a wedding was now guardian to a two year old and a four year old—and he was no help.

Christian turned on the shower and let it warm.

He'd been so overwhelmed with losing his best friend he'd nearly lost his mind. And it wasn't losing him. It was watching him die and not being able to get free from the accident to help him.

Just the thought of it made his heart kick start again.

He slipped off his boxers and climbed into the shower. No matter how hot the water was, it would never wash away the pain that day still caused.

By six thirty, he was dressed and sitting in his quiet kitchen having a cup of coffee. The dress shirt and tie made him uncomfortable, but it was the way he had to dress for work now. He supposed he owed it to his brother and uncle for stepping in and giving him a job, though he didn't care much about construction.

His entire family had stepped in when he needed them. There was no way to repay them. His sister Clara and cousin Avery were at his house daily to make sure he ate. His mother stopped by and cleaned the house. His future sister-in-law Darcy made him freezer dinners and stocked them for him.

It had been like this for a year.

When would it all ease so he could get on with his life?

Before lunch, the door to his office creaked open and Darcy stuck her head in.

"I'm going to lunch with my bridesmaids. Ed is free for Chinese food. He said to send you his way when you're done."

Christian nodded. "I'll be done in a few."

Darcy shut the door and Christian was alone, again. It was funny, he thought, for being so alone all the time there were always people around him. That was what came with a big family.

A new Chinese restaurant had opened just down the street and Ed had been dying to try it. Christian figured it would be good for leftovers and that it would warm up easily for dinner. It was just one less thing to think about.

"So did you look over that proposal I sent you?" Ed asked as he adjusted the place setting in front of him.

"Yeah. I don't know if I understand any of it. Could you work in some baseball terms?"

Ed laughed. "It's a baseball stadium. I thought you'd want to be part of that."

Christian put down his menu. "You'd think huh?"

He lazily looked around the restaurant and that was when a set of dark eyes caught his.

Victoria waved and was already walking toward them.

It had been nearly eight months since he'd seen her—since he'd told her that he wasn't someone who could just take on someone else's children and start from there. That was the day she walked out of his life. God, he was an idiot.

She looked different. Her hair was shorter and there were dark circles under her eyes, as if she hadn't slept in eight months. He probably looked like that too. He never got a good night's sleep.

"Hello, Chris." She smiled down at him and then turned her smile to Ed. "Hi, Ed."

"Tori!" Ed crawled out of the booth and gave her a hug. "How are you?"

"I'm good." Christian wondered if she noticed her voice quivered.

"How are the kids?"

Christian watched as her jaw tightened and she kept her eyes on Ed. "Sam just turned three last weekend. He's into everything. Ali just started kindergarten."

"Wow." Ed looked at Christian. "Kids get big fast, eh, Chris?"

Christian narrowed his stare on his brother.

"You'll be at the wedding right?" Ed was touching her arm. "I thought Darcy said you'd RSVP'd."

"I wouldn't miss it for the world. Ali can't stop talking about it."

"I look forward to it." Ed smiled and then both of them looked at Christian still seated in the booth.

"Guess we'll see you then," he croaked out.

Victoria nodded and forced a smile. As she walked past him, limping just as he did now too, she put her hand on his shoulder. "It was good to see you, Chris."

Then, she was gone.

Ed sat back down and shook his head. "You're pathetic."

"Me? Why?"

"She's still in love with you."

"She is not. She dumped me."

"Because she had to."

"Had to?" He picked up his hot tea and burned the pads of his fingers and then his throat. But it was worth it.

Ed opened the package of chop sticks by his plate and tore the two wooden pieces apart. "She lost a lot that night. Her sister died. Her brother-in-law died. She got two kids to raise and has no parents to help her. She's all alone and all you could tell her was you weren't ready for a fully formed family. I didn't realize you were an asshole, until that day."

If Christian was the man he used to be, he'd be up from that table and have pulled his brother out of that side of the booth by his shirt collar. But as if to remind him that he wasn't an athlete any more, his knee throbbed and the pain shot up through his body.

"She didn't need me around when she was trying to get things taken care of."

"You're right. Six surgeries on your leg and two toddlers at home is a piece of cake. Why have the man you love getting in the way?"

Christian swallowed hard. He didn't need his brother poking at him. It had been a year and he felt bad enough.

Luckily, the food arrived just in time for his brother to shove some in his mouth and shut up. Christian, on the other hand, had lost his appetite.

He had become a pathetic loser and he'd lost the only thing that he'd ever cared about—Victoria.

He took another long, scalding sip of his tea. Maybe Ed's wedding would be the perfect place to apologize for being an ass.

It wasn't in him to be a father right now, but it didn't mean he couldn't be a friend. She looked as though she certainly could use one. And they'd been friends too—hadn't they?

Christian tore open his chop sticks and broke them apart. As he picked up a pot sticker, he thought about his parents.

They'd been divorced when his mother was diagnosed with cancer and her husband had walked out on her to marry another woman and have a baby. She was alone with three kids.

He tugged at his collar because it was getting hot.

His own father, who was at the time engaged to Kathy, still stepped up and took care of his mother. Damn, he'd even shaved his head for her.

That was love. That was commitment.

It was right too. His father's marriage to Kathy lasted less than a day and he was back with Christian's mom and had been married, again, ever since.

What had Christian done when the woman he loved needed him? He backed away.

He put down the pot sticker. Again, he wasn't hungry.

They'd both lost a lot that night when that drunk driver hit that car. Lives changed in a flash—a bright white flash.

Ed was right. He was pathetic.

But he was done being pathetic. It was time Christian Keller took his life back—and the woman he still loved.

Chapter Two

Weekends had once been for playing ball. Then, they became time to chill with Victoria. One day they became two more days to sit still on the couch and wallow in the misery of what life had handed him. But Chris had decided he was done with that.

After seeing Tori, he wanted normalcy back.

Saturday morning, he looked around the living room and admired the view. The curtains had been open for the first time in months. A breeze blew through the open window and he could smell fresh cut grass. Spring time was a good time to start over.

Avery had tapped on the door, he'd seen her pull up, but then she pushed it open and walked right inside.

Her hands were full of grocery bags and she stopped and looked around.

"A little spring cleaning?"

Chris nodded tucking his thumbs into the front pockets of his jeans.

"I don't think I've ever seen this place look this nice. Tell me you got the ring out of your toilet too."

"Don't give me crap."

"Hard not to. Here help me with these." She hoisted a bag in his direction.

"I can go to a grocery store you know."

"I know, but seeing as you never do, I brought you some food so you won't starve."

Avery walked through the living room and back to the kitchen where she stopped again. "Chris, this looks great."

"Y'all have been taking care of me for too long. I thought it was time to get off of my sorry ass and sweep."

"There's more to that." She set the bags on the table. "Windows are open. There's fresh air in here. What is that?" She walked over to a small cup on the counter. "Is this a dandelion?"

He laughed as he placed the bags on the table next to the ones she had set there. "He was an early bloomer. I didn't have any flowers around to spruce up the joint."

Avery turned, crossed her arms over her chest, and narrowed her stare on him. "What gives?"

Not much had ever slipped past his cousin. There was no reason to keep it from her now. "I saw Tori the other day."

"Yeah, and Ed says you weren't very nice."

Christian rubbed his hand over the back of his neck. "I haven't been too nice to anyone." He waited for a comeback, but she didn't offer one. "I can't be a father to those kids. I think I'd be a lousy husband. But she really looked like she could use a friend."

"And you?"

He let out a breath. "I could use one too."

"Hallelujah, I think we might have cured you."

He grunted. "Don't get cocky. I might crawl back into bed tomorrow and stay there for a week."

She studied him. "Nah, I think you're going to be just fine."

Yeah, he just might. But he had a long road ahead of him. He wasn't truly happy working at Benson, Benson, and Hart, his uncle's construction firm. Chris had never been an Erector Set kind of kid. Always, he'd been the boy with a bat and glove.

"Who are you taking to Ed's wedding?" Chris asked as he peeked through the groceries and pulled out a bag of Doritos.

"Just that guy Paul from college."

"Paul? Gay Paul?"

"Safe date, right?"

"Sounds good to me. Thought he had a boyfriend."

"He does, but I'm not much of a threat." She laughed. "It looks like you don't need help with anything today. I guess I'll head out."

Chris pulled open the bag of chips. "You don't have to hurry out."

"I have a last fitting on my dress for the wedding. And then Darcy is taking us out to lunch."

"Ah, girlie things?"

"And my mom arranged for a limo to pick us all up and take us to a spa." Her faced glowed with excitement.

His Aunt Simone had been born into wealth and luxury. When he'd first met her, she screamed oil heiress.

But Avery's grandfather had taken away her wealth when Simone became pregnant with Avery out of wedlock. To add insult to injury the Parisian heiress was in love with a common American. Even as a young man Christian remembered when the woman, who once strutted around in designer clothes and high heels with her fingernails perfectly manicured, struggled to make ends meet. Simone had taken a simple job, moved in with a stranger, and learned that there were many others who could use a helping hand.

He pushed his shoulders back a little more. If a Parisian oil heiress could learn humility, so could he. Sure, his aunt eventually got her trust fund back and Avery would never need for anything, but there she was, in his kitchen unpacking the groceries she'd bought with her own measly paycheck. Her long black hair was up in a ponytail, or a knot, or something he'd seen girls do when they didn't care how they looked. But Avery Keller still looked beautiful.

"What's going on in that head of yours?" She asked opening his refrigerator, taking out an Izzy and opening it.

"Just thinking about how happy everyone around me is. My brother is getting married. My sister *is* married and is living on a tour bus." He licked the Dorito dust from his fingers. "You have a great new job. Spencer graduates college soon…" he stopped.

"And Ty is M.I.A." She set the drink on the counter.

Christian felt the ache in his gut. "No one has heard from him?"

"I think Spencer has, but he won't break that brother confidentiality."

Christian understood that bond. He had that with Ed. But the fact that his cousin had up and left to "find himself" still didn't sit well with the close knit Kellers.

His self-help time was completely understood. Christian was sure that if a woman came into his life claiming to be his sister that he'd never known about, he too would have to flee.

They all knew Tyler would come around. The question was when. After all, it was his long lost sister who was getting married to Ed. Wouldn't Tyler want to be there for that?

Avery pulled her cell phone out of her pocket and checked the time before picking her drink back up and taking a sip.

"So who are you taking to the wedding?"

"No one."

"Why not?"

"I haven't been too social lately. Can't think that anyone would want to go with me."

She nodded. "I hear Tori's going to be there—with the kids," she added quickly.

"I heard that too." He folded the top of the Dorito bag over and set it on the table. "Thought maybe it would be my opportunity to amend things. You never know where it could lead."

Avery studied him and then pursed her lips. This meant she knew something. He'd seen her make that face many times.

"What's up? You know something."

She shook her head and sipped from her can again. "It's nothing. I need to get going."

"Now your cheeks are flushing. You're lying."

"I am not," she started toward the door.

"Avery," his voice resonated his desperation.

She turned around and dropped her shoulders. "Tori marked the RSVP card that she was bringing the kids and a date."

The thought that she might bring a date or even that she might have someone in her life had never crossed Chris's mind. It was completely possible that Tori had moved on.

Suddenly the smell of fresh cut grass was a bit too much to take. Chris waited for Avery to leave and then he closed all the windows and pulled all the blinds.

Chapter Three

Nashville couldn't be lacking in spring wedding attire, but every store Victoria looked in, she was sure the town was dry.

She hated leaving the kids with a sitter, but she had to find a dress—the right dress. A knock-your-socks-off dress. But it didn't look as though it was going to happen.

Stuck in the back of her closet she had a dress she loved. Once upon a time it had been her favorite.

Chris had bought it for her one day. Okay, she admitted to herself, not just one day. The day. The very day he proposed to her.

She pushed through yet another rack of unappealing dresses. There was no way she'd show up to his brother's wedding wearing her own engagement dress. It was time to put the thought of Christian Keller out of her head. He wasn't the man she thought he was and she didn't have time to waste pining on him.

Scott Foster had been asking her out for months and she'd finally accepted, on the terms that he'd attend the wedding with her and the kids. He'd graciously accepted.

Scott understood the world she'd been thrust into. He was caring for his ailing mother, but he knew what it was to become care taker of someone you never thought you'd have to take care of. Christian Keller, on the other hand, couldn't even seem to take care of himself.

Victoria pushed aside yet another dress and let out a breath. Maybe it was a mistake to even go to the wedding. Darcy and Ed would understand, wouldn't they? It was just too hard. It just couldn't happen. It...

"Tori!"

She spun around at the calling of her name to see Christian's mother and sister hurrying toward her.

She didn't have to try and smile—it came naturally.

Clara was already within a few steps of her holding out her arms and enveloping her in a hug.

"Oh, I've missed you," she said as she hugged her tightly.

"How could you even have time? I saw you on the TODAY show last week. You and Warner have really made a name for yourself."

There was a pride that resonated from Clara and the excitement was infectious.

"It has been the craziest year and a half ever." Her face softened. "How are you?"

"I'm doing well."

Madeline, Christian's mother, stepped between them. "My turn." She pulled her into her arms and now Victoria was sure she might cry. "I've been thinking of you."

She pulled her back and kept her hands on Tori's arms to look her over. "You look beautiful. What are you shopping for?" she asked finally dropping her hands.

There was no way she was going to tell them her dilemma. Nope. She was going to make up something. These women didn't need her getting all emotional. It wasn't going to happen.

"A dress for the wedding," the words rushed out of her mouth before her contemplation of the situation was over.

"I'm so glad you're still coming." Madeline smiled wide. "Clara and I are headed just a few doors down to get our final fittings with the other girls. You should spend the day with us and we'll find you a dress."

"Oh, I couldn't even think of it."

Clara's lips turned into a pout. "You have to. I miss you."

"The kids are at a sitter."

"I'm sure she wouldn't mind. Oh, Tori, please. I haven't had the chance to pal around in a long time and this is the only girlie day I've had in months. It wouldn't be the same without you."

Victoria had never been good with the guilt—never.

"I suppose I could call the sitter and…"

But the words never got out. Clara had her in another hug and Victoria couldn't help but smile. She certainly did miss his family.

When Victoria walked through the doors of the bridal store with Madeline and Clara, the others were already there waiting. The reception she received from Chris's cousin Avery and Darcy was much the same as she'd received from Clara. Then his aunts, Regan, Arianna, and Simone embraced her as though she'd been the missing part in their lives for the past year.

She wasn't sure she was going to make it through the day without breaking down.

Her friend Sonia had told her to enjoy her day and that the kids were perfectly fine in her care. "I have three kids. Two more does not upset the balance in this house a bit," she told her. "You deserve a day with women who care about you. If I see you before five o'clock tonight I'm locking you out," she'd laughed. "Tori, go have fun."

She couldn't argue with that. It had been Sonia's strength that had helped her though the past year. Perhaps she was as close to a replacement sister as she could hope for, but that thought tugged at her chest too.

Clara set a hand on her shoulder. "Are you okay?"

"This is a bit emotional for me," she whispered.

Clara gave her a squeeze. "He's an idiot, but you'll always be one of my dearest friends. Don't forget that."

Victoria pressed her lips together tightly. "I won't."

The bridal store attendant set them all in an enormous fitting room. It was as if they were having a private party in the store. There was champagne, strawberries, and a whole lot of laughter.

Each bridesmaid tried on their dress and paraded around while the others applauded. The attendant made any adjustments that were needed and the next woman would go.

Victoria opted for one glass of champagne, but waved off the second when Clara offered.

Clara smiled and poured anyway. "Your day has just begun." She leaned in closer. "You're not driving for hours anyway. We have a surprise for Darcy and you're coming along."

Victoria's stomach filled with the unwelcomed nausea that came when butterflies invaded. Sonia said to stay away and the kids were safe and happy. She sat back in her chair and tried to accept the warmth she was being surrounded by, but it was all going to come at such an emotional price later.

Darcy was the last to try on her dress and tears flowed from Regan and Simone. Arianna shook her head at the two, but then turned and dabbed at her own eyes. Victoria, on the other hand, could feel the unwelcome onset of a full-on tearful breakdown coming.

As everyone in the room gushed over the bride, Victoria quietly slipped away to the bathroom. She couldn't do this. She couldn't spend the day with these women knowing that once, this day would have been hers.

She locked the door to the stall, took a handful of toilet paper, and began dabbing at her eyes.

"Tori, are you in here?" Clara had come after her and now she felt even worse.

She swallowed hard trying to steady her voice before she spoke. "I'll be just a moment."

"I can wait."

No, that's not what Victoria wanted. "You can go back. They need you."

But she didn't hear the door open again so she knew that Clara wasn't going anywhere.

When she felt composed she plastered a smile on her face and opened the door to the stall.

"Why are you crying?" Clara asked and that started the tears again.

"This is too hard. I don't think I can go on with you all today. I think I'd better go get the kids and go home."

Clara shook her head and walked toward her.

"Don't let him break you like this. He's hurting too."

"It was his choice."

Clara's brows drew together. "It was a stupid choice."

Victoria sucked in a breath. "No. It's a lot to throw at someone. The kids aren't his. There isn't a reason in the world that he should want to take on that responsibility."

"And you should have? Alone?"

"Well, they are mine."

Clara shook her head again. "In blood. Chris is yours in heart. That's equal."

Victoria dabbed at her eyes and kept the smile plastered on her tight lips. "No. He needs to heal in his own way. I needed to move on."

Clara took a step back. "I want you to stay. I want you to be part of our party. Don't let Chris ruin this."

"I'm a mess."

Clara laughed. "No, that would be Aunt Regan. Did you see how she blubbered out there?"

That finally gave way to a chuckle from Victoria. "I miss having you around." She cleared her throat. "Especially since my sister is gone."

Clara pulled her to her again. "I'll always be here, even if my buffoon of a brother is out of the picture." She gave her a squeeze and stepped back. "Okay, you get yourself together. Darcy is getting changed and we found a dress we think you should wear."

"Me?"

"Yeah, so hurry out."

Clara left the bathroom and Victoria stood there trying to compose herself. She'd so wanted to be one of the Keller women. They were strong and united together. Perhaps she was one after all.

She looked in the mirror at the woman she hardly recognized anymore. As she moved closer to the mirror she tried not to limp when she saw herself do so in the reflection, but it was near impossible. Her eye lids drooped and there were dark circles shadowing the blue eyes Chris had said he'd fallen in love with. Her blonde hair hung over her shoulders.

She set her purse on the counter and fetched out the small brush she kept there. After a few swipes through her hair she dug around for some lip tint. Finally, she found something that had a hint of pink. After a few more moments of primping she thought she looked healthier. Now it was time to test her nerves. Could she keep it together long enough to spend the day with the Keller women?

All of the Keller women were sitting on the couches in the fitting room as Darcy finished changing out of her dress. Victoria would have like to have just slipped in, but they were obviously waiting for her.

"C'mon, we found a dress we think you'll love," Regan stood and reached out a hand to Victoria.

She took her hand and let Regan lead her to an open dressing room.

"What do you think?"

It was simple. It was exactly what she'd been looking for. It was another trigger to start the tears.

"I think it's wonderful."

Regan smiled as if she knew what she was going through. "Try it on and come show us. Darcy thought the size was right."

Victoria nodded with a smile as Regan turned and left her alone in the room.

Her hands trembled as she reached for the dress. Already she knew it was out of her price range, but what was a little dress up among friends?

She took off her yoga pants, which she realized she'd become accustom to. Maybe she should think about a new pair of jeans. Toeing off her ratty sandals, she realized she needed a pedicure. Was that the beginning of a hole in her old Victoria Secret panties? *Wow*, she thought. She'd really let herself go.

Victoria stripped off her shirt and pulled the dress off the hanger.

Darcy had been right on the size. The floral print was warm and full of spring time. The capped sleeves gave a graceful accent to her arms, which she'd always thought was her best feature. And the V-neck gave way to her delicate B-cups.

Victoria slowly opened the door to the dressing room to the room full of women whose conversation stalled as she walked out.

"Oh, Tori! It's perfect!" Darcy clasped her hands together. "That's it! That's the dress."

Victoria walked toward the large mirrors where all the women had stood in their dresses. The dress was flattering and sophisticated—and fun.

Simone walked up behind her and gave a few tugs on the fabric. "It fits so well, I don't think it even needs altering," she said in her beautiful French accent, which Victoria adored.

"It's very nice. I don't think I can afford it though."

The women again went silent.

Darcy walked toward her and took her hands. "We are all pitching in and buying you the dress. It's a gift."

"Oh, no. I can't…"

"It's already done. And look at this." Darcy turned around and pointed to Madeline who held a smaller version of the dress. "There's one for Ali."

That was the final straw. The tears gave no notice before they fell freely down her cheeks.

"Really, you all don't have to…"

"We all want to." Darcy brushed a tear from her own cheek. She leaned in to Victoria. "You're supposed to be my sister-in-law. Just because he's a freaking moron doesn't mean I have to lose that," she whispered.

Victoria pressed her fingers to her lips to keep them still.

She *was* a Keller woman. She would just have to do without the Keller man.

Chapter Four

Christian adjusted the tie that currently suffocated him. He hated the monkey suit. His brother was getting married—not him. Why did he have to be formal for dinner? Really...it was going to be his family and Darcy's dad and he needed a suit?

"Stop fidgeting." Clara walked up and adjusted the tie he'd just loosened. "Are you sick or something? You're sweating."

He rubbed the scar on his forehead when it began to itch, as it did when he'd get hot. "I don't want to be here."

"I worry about you. You always were a quiet kid, but since the accident you've been shut off from the world. We all still exist you know."

Christian grit his teeth. "I'm just nervous. It's been a long time since I stood in front of a lot of people and had to talk. Giving speeches is not my forte."

"You're going to be fine." She patted him on the shoulder. "And to think two years ago you were a cocky ball player."

She walked away, but the sting of her words had done their job. She was right. He'd been a quiet, almost shy, kid. Then he'd become the epitome of the jock. Full of himself and easy with the ladies. And then came Tori.

Okay, he had to admit it—the real issue at hand was knowing he had to face Tori tomorrow. Seeing her had been one thing. Knowing she was bringing a date had twisted him up. And then to top it off, all Clara and Avery could talk about all week was about the day they had with her. They'd bought her a dress and took her to lunch. After that, Simone had surprised Darcy with a limo and a spa day—in which they'd included Tori

He knew she was going to knock his socks off tomorrow. She was going to take that wedding by storm. And she was going to do it all with another man at her side.

Christian clenched his fists to his side. He'd turned her away, why did it hurt so bad to think about her?

With two beers and a glass of champagne already floating in his system, Chris sat down for dinner next to his sister. Thank God for bread, because once they passed around another flute of champagne he was expected to stand up and give a nice speech. Worse, he was expected to do it again tomorrow night—a different speech.

Clara patted his arm. "You're up."

Chris's mouth went dry and he licked his lips as he stood. He was supposed to be prepared, but he wasn't. Couldn't Warner, his professional performing brother-in-law, give the speech?

He cleared his throat. "Ed and Darcy. Well, we made it to this day. I don't know about you, but it seems as though you've been planning it forever." Everyone laughed and he loosened the tie his sister had tightened again. "I love you both and I'm so glad you found each other." He cleared his throat again. "Darcy, you are a wonderful addition to our family. And I don't just mean our little family. I mean all of the Keller/Benson family." He watched her dab a tear from her eye. "Ed, you're a pain in the ass." Again, everyone laughed. "But I can't think of a stronger man I'd like to follow though in this life." He held his glass high. "The best to you both—forever."

Everyone applauded and sipped their drink. Chris noticed his hand shook and he downed the golden liquid just to numb himself.

It was then he was reprieved from being the center of attention when his cousin Tyler walked through the door.

The gasps and sobs continued as Regan flew from her seat and toward her son who, almost two years earlier had abandoned the family, to find himself, after learning that Darcy was the sister he'd never known about.

Christian sat back down in his chair and let the room swarm around Tyler. He was much more comfortable with that. He'd take his moment with him. He understood feeling lost. But Chris had to admit, he was glad to see him again.

Tyler joined them for dinner in the private dining room and Christian was able to relax into his chair and no one seemed to notice him.

After dessert, he took his glass of water out onto the veranda and watched the people who gathered under the atrium.

"You look far away, cuz." Tyler slapped a hand on Chris's shoulder and left it there.

"It's nice to see you."

Tyler rested his arms on the railing and looked down at the people below as Chris was doing. "I'm not quite ready to come back."

"Everyone misses you."

"I'm dying not being around everyone." He turned and leaned against the railing looking into the room where their family celebrated. "I've really tried to think about what my mom was going through when Darcy was born. For Darcy's sake, she did the right thing by giving her up for adoption."

"So what's holding you back from forgiving her completely and coming home?"

Tyler shrugged. "She kept it from us and that hurts. I get it, God, I get it. But…"

"I know." Chris turned and leaned against the railing next to his cousin. "If you do decide to come back I have a lot of space in my house. You're welcome to stay."

Tyler chuckled. "So you and Tori?"

"Old news."

"I'm sorry to hear that. She was something really special."

Didn't he know it? He thought about the hotel they stood in, and the memory of their first date played in his head. They'd gone to his Aunt Simone's fundraiser and his best friend had set him up with his sister-in-law. It hadn't taken long for him to fall in love with Tori. Making it even funnier was the thought that he'd met Darcy that night too.

Chris sipped his water. "I can't be a father to her niece and nephew. I'm still trying to wrap my head around what has happened in my life in the past few years."

"It can only get better, right?"

He hoped so.

Tyler moved from the railing. "Well, even if things don't work out in the forever department, maybe you can still be friends."

"That's what I'm hoping for."

"And who knows, maybe I'll take you up on that extra space."

Tyler gave him a nod and went back into the room with their family.

Chris let out a steady breath. He'd already decided that friendship was possible. Yeah, he'd start with that.

~*~

Victoria looked in the mirror and turned her head from side to side. She hadn't realized how much she'd let herself go over the past year, until she'd been spoiled with a facial and an eyebrow wax. Even nearly a week later, she still looked refreshed. She studied her manicure. She'd managed to keep it intact too.

Sonia looked at the dress that hung in the doorway to the bathroom. "I can't believe they bought you a dress for the wedding."

"Look at the price tag. That would have set me back a month."

"It wasn't about the price, Tori."

"I shouldn't even be going to this wedding. This is all crazy." She pulled her hair into a tail on the top of her head and wrapped a band around it. "I don't belong with them anymore."

Sonia shook her head. "It would kill you not to go. Besides, I expect to see a picture of Christian in a tux."

The image was seared in her mind of what he looked like in—and out of—a tux.

Sonia leaned against the doorjamb. "So you're taking Scott?"

"Uh-huh."

"Couldn't you find someone safer?"

Victoria laughed and turned to her friend. "Safer? Why do I want safe? I want sturdy and reliable. I want employed and well balanced. I want a father figure for the kids. Safe? I'm trying to move on. This is just a few hours away from the reality that the best man isn't mine anymore. So I think Scott is as safe as it gets."

Sonia held up her hands as if to surrender. "Got it. I'd better head home and take my monkeys before they get your two more riled up."

Sonia turned and headed down the hallway to collect her kids from the family room. Victoria followed, yawning as she stepped over toys which had been scattered through the house.

Sonia's kids gathered their things and they headed toward the door.

"Listen—if you need me you call me. You don't owe Scott anything and you certainly don't owe Chris anything either. You're going to be there for Darcy and Ed. But if you or the kids need an escape you call me."

"I will."

"I mean it."

Victoria smiled. "I promise."

Sonia kissed Victoria on the cheek and headed out to the minivan in the driveway.

Victoria closed the door and rested her back against it. She looked at her home, now a mess with toys and mismatched clothing items. It would all keep until after the wedding. They were all going to need their beauty rest for tomorrow—and their strength.

Chapter Five

The hallway of the church was full of men and each of them were pacing in different directions. Ed, the one who *should* be pacing, stood in the center of the room like an anxious child waiting for a candy store to open.

Carlos, their father, had just helped his parents into the church. Darcy's father wrung his hands together until Clara poked her head out of the room down the hall and signaled for him. Regan, Simone, and Arianna walked out of the room with wide grins on their faces. They each grabbed their husbands and found their seats.

Spencer and Tyler continued to seat late guests and then took their places by the door.

Madeline was the last to leave the room and she was already wiping tears from her eyes. "Give me just one more moment, okay?" she said patting Ed's cheek and hurrying to the restroom.

Ed turned to Clara's husband Warner. "You know you should have to deal with her when she's like this. You took the chicken way out of it by eloping."

"You're right. But we did end up with a few silent dinners because of it."

Ed grinned and turned to Chris, who continued to pace. "You look more nervous than I do."

"You look nervous."

"I do not."

"Okay, you're right. Why aren't you nervous?"

Ed pushed back his shoulders. "I love her. I love her like I can't imagine ever loving anyone else in my whole life."

Chris swallowed hard. "I'm really happy for you."

Just then, their mother walked out of the restroom. "This is as good as it's going to get."

"Mom, I think you look wonderful."

The minster appeared from the chapel. "We are ready."

The men followed him down the aisle and Ed escorted his mother to her seat. He kissed her on the cheek and then did the same to his father before joining Chris and Warner.

Warner's guitar waited on a stand beside him. When he was given the signal by his wife, he picked up the guitar and began to play.

Chris watched the door at the back of the church, careful not to look around. He wasn't ready to meet the eyes of anyone—specifically Tori's date.

The guests turned in their seats and that was when Chris saw the flower girl and the ring bearer walk down the aisle with Avery's gentle instructions being whispered to them.

Christian leaned toward Ed. "When did Ali and Sam become part of your wedding?" he asked quietly through gritted teeth.

"Last night," Ed whispered. "Darcy wanted it."

Chris fisted his hands to his side and finally looked around at the guests.

Seated on the bride's side of the church was Tori. She was only three rows away from him, but he hadn't seen her when he walked in.

Seeing her there, turned around, taking pictures of her niece and nephew, he felt like bursting into a fit of tears himself. They were beautiful and she was obviously so proud of them.

He appreciated her for a moment as she was turned from him. The beautiful dress the women had bought her exposed her sculpted shoulders and her long, soft neck. Small pearls dangled from her ears—pearls he'd given her.

Blonde curls cascaded over her shoulders and he thought of the many times he'd brushed those strands away so he could kiss every inch of her delicate skin.

His memories were quickly shattered when the man seated next to her grasped her hand in his and she turned to smile at him, still beaming as if those kids were theirs.

The realization of the moment hurt. Perhaps that's what was going on. This man had been the man to step in and take on that heavy burden with her.

As Ali and Sam made it to the front of the sanctuary and Tori turned, his eyes locked with hers. A million painful emotions bounced between them as they kept each other's gaze.

Would she ever know how sorry he was?

At that moment he certainly knew how sorry he was— and it was selfish.

As the guests stood when Darcy and her father entered the sanctuary, Christian's eyes were diverted from Tori. Not by the amazing vision in white walking toward his brother who was grinning like a fool, but because the man with Tori had stood and wrapped his arm protectively around her waist.

There were a million videos that had gone viral on the internet where the best man had fallen over—Chris wondered how many of them started with a guilt ridden man wishing away all the hurtful words he'd said to a woman.

As Darcy passed by Tori's pew, Christian was sure to turn away and look toward his brother.

Ed's eyes were wide and the smile on his mouth had actually grown wider.

Christian looked at Darcy. She was absolutely breath taking. He swallowed hard. Not once had he considered that he might cry at this wedding. He wasn't supposed to be sentimental about it. He'd cried when his parents remarried, but that made sense.

Quickly he batted away the first tear as the minister asked who gave the bride to the groom. When her father answered, he lifted Darcy's veil and kissed her on the cheek before shaking Ed's hand.

And with that, the ceremony began and soon his brother was married.

Christian looked at his sister, who sobbed like a child. A glance at Warner and he literally felt his knees wobble. There was a gaze going between them that said they were happy together and that they loved each other.

Watching his brother kiss his new bride, Chris felt the pang of regret and jealousy mix in his chest.

He so badly wanted to turn and look at Tori. He wanted to know if they still had that connection, but he was afraid to. What if he turned and she was looking at that man in the same way his brother and sister looked at their spouses?

Giving his knees a slight bend he stood there applauding until it was time to give his sister his arm and escort her back down the aisle following their brother.

Victoria madly dabbed at her eyes with her handkerchief hoping that her makeup hadn't run down her face and that perhaps there was a little of it left.

Ali and Sam had been so cute walking down the aisle, she'd never had a chance to even try and keep her emotions intact.

Scott rested his hand atop hers. "Are you going to be okay?"

"I cry at weddings. It's my curse."

He patted her hand. "It's perfectly acceptable."

The pews were emptying out and Scott took her hand, interlaced their fingers, and they followed the guests out to the front of the church where the bride and groom would greet everyone.

Ali and Sam broke free of Avery's hands the moment they saw her. Sam ran to her quickly and she knelt down to scoop him up. "You did a good job."

"Rings!" He grinned.

"That's right."

"Did you see all of my flowers?" Ali stood next to her looking up at her.

"I did! Did you have fun?"

Ali nodded enthusiastically.

Victoria looked up and noticed the reception line was moving along. Suddenly the nerves which had sickened her all morning now threatened to kill her in that line. Avery met guests with Spencer. Tyler seemed to have slipped away and she wondered if she should find him just to give her an excuse to leave the line as well.

Warner and Clara were the next to greet guests and Clara scooped up Ali and held her on her waist.

"I think Darcy made the right choice when she decided on a flower girl."

"She said I can keep the basket too," Ali said.

"She sure did." Clara set Ali down on the ground. "Thank you for letting them do this on such short notice."

"They were thrilled," she squeaked out as Clara's husband Warner stepped out of the receiving line, leaving Christian exposed to her.

He glanced at her out of the corner of his eye, but an older woman had him deep in conversation—or was giving him an earful of her conversation.

"Let me take him," Scott said reaching for Sam who easily went to him.

With Ali between them they took a step toward Christian at the same moment Scott slid his arm around her waist.

Victoria's breath caught in her lungs. Scott knew nothing of Christian. He was an innocent party to the deceiving reason she'd invited him to the wedding. But she couldn't have faced the Kellers alone. Christian had kicked her and her newly inherited family to the curb, figuratively of course.

She'd gone out with Scott a few times over the past month and he was a nice and gentle man. He hadn't been too forward. Not once had he suggested she let him spend the night or ditch the kids and stay with him. They'd shared a few heated kisses, though they were weak in comparison to even the memory of Christian's kisses. But Scott was mentally healthy and happy. He loved the kids. There were so many positives. The only negative about him—he wasn't Christian Keller.

The woman who had been talking to Christian moved on to embrace Darcy and kiss both of her cheeks and he turned to look at her.

"Hello, Tori."

She swallowed the lump in her throat. "Hello, Chris."

"I heard all about this dress. You look lovely."

She'd noticed that he'd never even looked at the dress. His eyes were firm on hers.

"I'm Scott Foster."

Scott held his hand out to Christian and she saw Christian's jaw tighten.

"Christian Keller, brother of the groom."

"Nice to meet you. It was a very nice wedding."

"It was perfect wasn't it?" Darcy offered resting a hand on Christian's shoulder. "Tori, you look beautiful."

She pulled her into an embrace and then pulled back to look at her.

Victoria felt her cheeks heat. "You were all too kind to buy me the dress."

"And thank you for letting me use the kids." Darcy knelt down among the many layers of her dress to be at Ali's height. "You were the perfect flower girl."

"I can keep the basket right?"

Darcy smiled. "You can."

"Rings!" Sam said loudly still perched on Scott's hip.

Darcy stood. "And you did wonderful too." She lifted on her toes to kiss his cheek before extending her hand toward Scott. "I'm Darcy Keller...Oh, doesn't that sound cool?"

Ed wrapped his arm around Darcy's shoulders. "Most perfect name ever." He kissed her on the cheek and held his hand out to Scott. "Eduardo Keller."

"Scott Foster."

Victoria looked to Scott's side and realized that at some point Christian had slipped away. She pressed her hand to her stomach where she was sure a lead ball had dropped.

They'd pleasantly made it though the rest of the line and she'd introduced Scott to everyone along the way. It had been perfect Keller charm too—not one of them giving her pity or making Scott feel unwelcomed. In fact, if Chris himself didn't say anything, Scott might never know what the family meant to her at all.

They walked to the car and strapped the kids into their seats. When Victoria sat in her seat and latched the seat belt, Scott looked at her.

"It was a nice wedding," he said starting the engine.

She closed her eyes and rested her head against the back of the seat. "It sure was."

Scott backed out of the parking lot and headed toward the Opryland Hotel. "You're pretty close with the Kellers, huh?"

"Yeah," she said on a sigh.

"Christian Keller? He was a ball player with your brother-in-law, right?"

Victoria licked her lips to moisten her mouth. "Uh-huh."

Scott reached for her hand and interlaced their fingers. He ran his thumb over hers in the most intimate of gestures and Victoria thought of how sweet they must look—this family dressed in their best, very cozy in Scott's Lexus.

She let the tension roll out of her shoulders.

Scott gave her a glance and then turned his eyes back to the road. "So how long did you and Christian Keller date?"

The tension was back, but this time it stiffened every muscle in her body. The weight in her stomach was back too and it literally made her sick. She knew she'd tightened the grip she had on Scott's hand.

"What makes you think we dated?"

He chuckled and continued to stroke her hand with his thumb. "The way he complimented your dress without looking at it. The grip he used when shaking my hand. The awkwardness you didn't have with anyone else. Should I go on?"

"Please don't." She rolled her head to the side to look at him. He was handsome—more rugged than Christian with strong features and a dark completion. He was a natural in a suit—where she'd seen Christian squirm. There was an athletic build under that Armani and she'd seen it. They'd taken the kids swimming at his condo building last week. It had been the first time she'd been in a swim suit in over a year, but he hadn't looked at the scars that riddled her body. He'd made her feel secure in her own skin.

Victoria took a breath. "We dated up until about eight months ago."

He nodded and guilt plagued her.

"Okay, we didn't just date. We were engaged."

His thumb stopped moving against hers for a moment "It would have been nice to know I was being thrown into the lion's den."

"I know." She slouched in her seat. "I'm so sorry."

He smiled. "It's okay. I'm a lawyer, remember. I'm used to the den."

"But it wasn't fair of me to do that to you."

"So why aren't you and the awkward groomsman married?"

It would be easy to throw Christian under the bus and make Scott hate him, but she didn't even hate him—though she wanted to.

"After the accident he just couldn't wrap his head around the loss and the injuries," she sighed. "And the kids."

"Your injuries?" His voice rose.

"His."

The light turned red and Scott stopped and looked at her. "His injuries? He was in the car with you?"

She nodded. "He was pinned behind Dave. He couldn't move. He couldn't save him."

Scott let out a long breath. "I didn't know."

"He'd already had injuries that had threatened his career, but the accident solidified that. In one moment he lost his best friend, his career, and the quiet life he thought we'd have. He just couldn't take on being a father."

When the light turned green Scott began to drive. "That family doesn't seem like the kind that wouldn't accept kids into it."

"It's not. It's a very eclectic family. Chris's dad is adopted as well as two of his aunts. Darcy is actually the daughter of his Aunt Regan, whom she gave up for adoption when she was born. She fell in love with Ed before they knew who she really was."

Scott's mouth pursed. "They're cousins?"

Victoria laughed. "On paper only I suppose. Regan was adopted and so was Carlos. And Darcy has a different father than Spencer and Tyler. So in blood they aren't related at all."

"It's a tad confusing."

She let out a little laugh. "I think it's beautiful."

He was silent until they saw the hotel come into view. "If you'd like to go back to the reception alone, I can take the kids out to a movie or something."

Victoria shot open her eyes and turned to him. "No."

"Are you sure?"

"Very."

Scott pulled into the lot and parked the car. As he turned off the engine she looked into the backseat. Both kids had fallen asleep. Their heads both leaned into the center toward each other.

"They are my life now," she said softly.

Scott turned and looked at them. A grin formed on his lips. "They're beautiful."

"I may never have any of my own."

"Why?" He turned to her and removed his dark sunglasses so she could see his dark eyes gazing at her.

Victoria shrugged. "No one wants a premade family."

Scott lifted his hand to her cheek. "That's not true."

She could feel her lips begin to quiver.

Scott moved in closer to her. "Some of us think that what you're doing is heroic. Unselfish. Sexy."

She nearly let out a snort. "Sexy."

"Mmm-hmm," he let it roll from his throat as he moved in closer, pressing his lips to hers.

The heat in the car rose a good ten degrees as he worked his lips against hers. The weight of the guilt had given into a million sputtering butterflies in her stomach.

When he pulled back, his dark eyes fixed on hers. "Offer still stands. I can give you some room and you can go do some flaunting in front of Christian Keller in that dress."

Victoria licked her lips, trying to savor the kiss. "I think I'd rather go in as a family."

The subtle smile that now played on his pinked lips gave her hope. Christian Keller needed to be replaced in her heart and in her life. Scott Foster seemed to be the man to make that happen.

She looked back as Ali opened her eyes. A few more hours and she'd step away from the Kellers and start a life without looking back.

The butterflies in her stomach must have all died, she thought as the weight of them plunged to the bottom and she felt ill.

Chapter Six

Christian wondered how a person could unsee something. There had to be a drug or a drink or an operation that could take away pain in your heart and make you forget that you'd seen the woman you loved, and had turned away, kissing another man in the parking lot.

He didn't like this Scott guy. She didn't go for the business man type. She was more of an athletic man's girl.

Christian clenched his fists tightly to his side. Well, she'd been his girl.

He watched from the front door of the hotel as she and Scott got out of the Lexus and each of them pulled a sleepy child out of the backseat. Ali rested her head on Scott's shoulder and Sam was still asleep as Tori pulled him to her.

They began to walk his way—he with a swagger—she with a limp. Every step she took looked as though it caused her pain. And yet she did it while carrying a child—her child now.

"Party is inside, pretty boy," Tyler slapped Chris on the back.

"I'm coming."

Tyler looked in the direction which Christian was looking. "Looks like she's moved on."

He'd never hit family before, but Tyler might have it coming. "He's temporary."

They both watched as Scott slid his arm around her waist and dipped down to give her a small kiss on the lips as they carried the kids toward the hotel.

"Hmmm," Tyler groaned. "It doesn't look temporary."

Christian turned and headed into the hotel with only one thing on his mind. Open bar.

The music was nice, he thought. The food was okay. The corner of the banquet hall he'd holed up in was dark enough to get lost in. He didn't know how many Jack and Cokes he had, but he knew he wasn't done.

He sipped his drink and watched as Scott held Tori tight on the dance floor as they looked down lovingly at the kids who danced beside them.

Tyler walked toward him and handed him a glass of water. "Maybe you'd better try one of these."

"I did that you know. I pushed her to him."

"Can I tell you from the perspective of someone who has taken a two year sabbatical from all of this to have a pity party—it's not worth what you're doing right now."

Christian looked up at him, taking a moment to focus through the haze. "I think I deserve a pity party. My leg hurts. My shoulder aches. This freaking scar on my head burns." He sipped the water. "And I gave that man a family."

"He looks happy."

That's what had been pissing him off the most. They did look happy.

He watched as Clara ran out onto the dance floor with Tori's cell phone and she put it to her ear. There was nodding and then she'd asked the kids something, to which they nodded and clapped. A moment later the four of them left the dance floor.

Clara, with her innate sense of his misery, found her way to the corner.

"Did you get him some water?" she asked Tyler.

"I did."

"Good." She turned and looked at the guests then pointed. "See that woman over there. The red head?"

"Who hasn't seen her?" Tyler asked.

Christian strained to see. He hadn't seen her, but by his cousin's dripping voice he must have been missing something good.

"She wants to meet Chris."

"Me?" He refocused on his sister.

"Yeah. But you're over here swaying to your own music."

He chuckled. He was swaying.

"Where did Tori go?"

Clara dropped her shoulders and gave him a grunt. "Sonia offered to take the kids so she and Scott could have a nice night together."

He grit his teeth and finished off the Jack and Coke in his other hand.

"So where is this red head?"

Victoria kissed Sonia on the cheek as Scott shut the door to the minivan.

"Thank you."

"My pleasure," Sonia smiled. "You think I'm doing you a favor. But your two keep my three occupied so I can get some housework done." She opened the door and slid into the van. "Listen, they *are* staying the night. I don't want to see your face on my step before ten in the morning. Understand me? This is some adult time." She gave her eyebrows a rise. "If you know what I mean."

Victoria already felt her hands begin to shake. "I'm not sure about that."

"You're too straight laced. Have some fun." Sonia looked toward Scott who waited patiently on the other side of the van. "He's easy on the eyes and very sweet on you."

Victoria hugged her dearest friend again. "I love you."

"I know. If Craig and I ever get a night alone you can take my kids." She winked at her and closed the door.

Scott waved as the minivan drove away. Victoria clasped her hands behind her back to keep them from visibly shaking in front of him.

"I have you all to myself, huh?" Scott wrapped his arms around her waist.

"I guess you do," her voice was much too airy.

"I won't make you uncomfortable. I promise." He pressed a gentle kiss to her lips. "All at your speed, okay?"

She nodded.

"C'mon," he said offering her his arm. "Let's go back inside and dance."

When they got to the base of the staircase Scott's cell phone rang. He pulled it from his pocket and grimaced when he saw the ID screen.

"I have to take this," he said apologetically.

"Go ahead. I'll wait for you on the veranda."

Victoria climbed the stairs alone, ducked into the reception and retrieved two glasses of champagne. She then went back out on the veranda which overlooked the atrium and waited for Scott.

It was nearly ten minutes before he joined her and she'd drank down half her flute of champagne.

As he walked toward her she noted the perplexed look on his face.

"Is everything okay?" she asked handing him the other flute.

"Josh Mason."

"The country singer?"

"Yeah, him."

"What about him?"

"He's my client. He's also a womanizing, party boy. Seems as though after a concert in South Carolina, he got a little drunk, took a drive, hit a car, and might have made a few moves on the wrong police woman."

"Oh." She tucked in her lips and studied him a moment longer. "What does this mean for you?"

"It means I have a flight in three hours."

Her eyes shot open. That wasn't what she was expecting. "You have to leave?"

He nodded and handed back the flute of champagne. "I have to go. I can take you home or…"

She looked into the room where music played. She didn't want to go home yet. "I'll ask Avery or Clara to drop me off. I'd like to stay if that's okay."

"It's more than okay." He pulled her to him and she splayed out her arms to avoid spilling the champagne. "I really had a nice time and I hope when I get back we can pick up where we left off."

"I'd like that."

Scott tilted his head and kissed her. It wasn't the calm and soft kisses he'd been giving her all day, this one had meaning and it said he wanted more. His tongue slipped between her lips and she inhaled through her nose sharply, and then relaxed against him, her arms still held out to the side.

When he pulled away his eyes were darker. "This sucks," he said with a grin before the chime on his phone directed his attention to a text message. "And here we go." He looked at his phone quickly. "I'll call you."

Victoria nodded and watched as Scott quickly descended down the stairs. She stood there alone with two flutes of champagne and a party within a few feet of her, but she didn't move. Instead she stood there looking out over the people that moved about in the atrium.

"Aren't you and your date going into the party?" The slurred speech was still too familiar.

Victoria turned around to see Christian behind her with a bottle of water in his hands. His tux coat had been discarded and his bow tie hung untied around his neck. He must have run his fingers through that dark mass of wavy hair enough times to create tunnels.

She swallowed the lump in her throat and took a breath to speak. "He had to leave."

"Stranded you at the prom?"

She nodded. "Something like that. But I can get a cab or call Sonia."

He took a few crooked steps toward her. "I'll get you home," he offered very sincerely.

She coughed. "You? Please tell me you have a ride home."

Christian dropped his shoulders. "Clara has my keys."

"Good. She's brilliant."

"She's a pain in my ass."

Victoria had to laugh at that, because she knew the Kellers too well. There wasn't anything that one wouldn't do for another.

He moved toward the railing where she stood. "You gonna drink both of those?"

She lifted the untouched glass and handed it to him, but he took the glass she'd been drinking from. "I'll take this one. You're far behind me on drinks."

He tapped the glass to hers and drank down what was left. Victoria took a long sip of hers and it went straight to her head.

She batted her eyes and Christian grinned. "You never were a big drinker."

"Neither were you."

"It's my crutch tonight." He balanced his hand on the railing. "Was kinda having a hard time."

"Because of Darcy?"

He crinkled up his expression. "Darcy? Why would I have a hard time with that?"

"Because you liked her."

"Oh, pftttt." He waved his hand through the air. "I liked that I lived in the same house with her and it pissed off my brother because he was in love with her. She took care of me when I needed it." His face became more somber. "It had nothing to do with Darcy."

As a waiter walked past with another tray of glasses, Christian exchanged the empty ones for full ones and handed Victoria a glass.

This time she drank down half of it in one drink.

"A little more relaxed?" he asked.

"Yeah." She needed to be. She didn't like being nervous around Chris.

They'd parted on terms that they'd remain friends. That's what she still wanted. This was the perfect opportunity to prove that she could just be his friend.

Christian moved in closer to her. "There are a lot of people in there having a good time."

"I see that."

"It seems silly for us to just stand in the hall and drink alone. Let's dance."

"Oh, Chris, I don't think…"

He brushed his fingers down the scar on her arm and it sent a shiver through her that had her gasping. "It's just a dance. Among friends."

She should have left with Scott. She should have never stayed alone at the wedding. What did she think? That she'd be okay with him there and her alone?

"Just friends," she reiterated and took Christian's offered arm.

They were a pair limping along side of each other into the room full of people. The lights were low, music played, people mingled.

They set their glasses on a table and Christian led her to the dance floor. He'd seen his mother elbow his father and point in their direction, but he pretended not to.

The rest of the Kellers would be vital in him making a move on her. They liked her—he still loved her. He didn't think he could be a father, but he sure as hell didn't want that Scott guy taking the job either.

As they stepped onto the dance floor the music changed, slowed, and the lights dimmed more. Christian wrapped his arm around Tori's waist and pulled her as close as he possibly could to him. She rested her hand on his shoulder and clasped her hand into his other.

They'd never danced well, but they were a pair with their limping and their scars. Still, they swayed together and he managed to get her even closer, until they were cheek to cheek.

"Did you pay the DJ to play this?" She said softly in his ear.

He finally listened to the song. Unchained Melody played and the verse, "Are you still mine? I need your love," rang in his ears.

"That would be giving me too much credit."

He'd noticed that her hand was no longer on his shoulder, but instead her arm was draped behind his neck. He pulled their clasped hands in closer until they were rested between them.

How was it that in a matter of minutes he had her pressed so close to him, swaying to a song that was so close to ending.

It was a sign, right? She had to miss him as desperately as he missed her. There was no other reason to be able to hold her so close.

One song melted into another slow dance and she stayed in his arms. In a bold move, he slid his hand from hers and laced it around her waist forcing her to take her other arm around his neck too. Now they were completely pressed together. Their cheeks rested against each other's and he was sure he could feel her fingertips massaging the nape of his neck.

He closed his eyes and breathed in her perfume. Chanel No. 5. He'd bought her a bottle at Christmas last year and she'd sworn she'd only wear it for special occasions. He couldn't think of a more special occasion than this one—and he didn't mean his brother's wedding.

Tori's breath was laboring, meaning she was feeling something between them. He could feel her heart racing since she was pressed so close to him.

Suddenly, the numerous Jack and Cokes and two glasses of champagne swam in his head.

"I think this going around in circles on the dance floor is making me more drunk than I already was. Take a walk through the atrium with me."

She pulled back enough that he could see her face. Her lips parted. Her eyes closed and opened again in a slow, sexy blink.

"Okay, and then I need to go home."

He nodded in agreement, but he had no plans on letting her leave his side for at least a few hours. Maybe a nice long walk would help sober him up so he didn't say or promise anything stupid. Right now he just wanted her close. He needed her. He'd missed her.

Chapter Seven

It seemed that Christian had sobered quite a bit before he quickly escorted her out of the room, but not before he'd grabbed two more glasses of champagne.

Victoria was sure she was making a mistake being alone with him. But for some reason, she didn't care. Perhaps it was the champagne.

This was what she'd wanted, wasn't it? She'd wanted to be with him and now she was.

He handed her a glass and tapped his against it. "To Ed and Darcy."

Victoria smiled. "To Ed and Darcy." She took a sip and blew out a breath. "I am getting just a little light headed with all this champagne."

Christian gave her a crooked grin that had one side of his mouth turning up. "I can't even see you clearly." He laughed. "But I know how you look and I know it's a picture of beauty."

Those butterflies were back in her stomach. She took another big sip of champagne to try and drown them.

"Are you sure you want to walk? I mean we can just stand here and talk. Or not," she offered. "We could just go sit."

"I'm just afraid you'll run out if I don't keep you occupied by dancing or walking."

"I don't do either one very well," she said with her voice dripping.

Christian blinked hard and then furrowed his brows. "How is your leg?"

She shrugged. "Horrible." Why lie to him? He knew pain. "They think I might need a few more surgeries. As it is, I'm just a walking scar statue."

"Can I see?"

She narrowed her eyes on him.

"Your leg. The scars."

There was a seriousness to him that made her know he wasn't making a play on her. She bit down on her lip and handed him her glass. Then she took a step back from him and slowly lifted the skirt on her dress to expose her leg.

His face showed concern. "And they want to do more?"

She nodded. "It's no big deal."

He shot his look up to her. "No big deal? It's a huge deal. How do you take care of the kids when…" he stopped and she knew he'd finally stumbled over his tongue.

"I have friends," she said dropping her skirt into place. "I'm not all alone." She took the glass from his hand and drank down the rest of it.

"I'm still your friend," he said, but his words slurred. Though, she wasn't sure if his words slurred or her hearing did.

"Friends don't just forget the other person when they need them the most."

She saw the fire light behind his eyes. "I didn't forget you."

"Really? I haven't heard from you in eight months. Not until I bumped into you at lunch." Her head was swimming, but at this point she didn't care. She finished off the drink.

"And you think it was because I didn't care?"

"I think it's because Christian Keller can't think of anyone but himself."

His mouth dropped open, but he didn't say anything.

Victoria decided that she needed to call Sonia and beg for a ride. As she started for the banquet room—now limping and swaying—Christian caught her hand.

"You promised me a walk."

"All about you." She pulled her hand back. "See what I mean?"

"Damn it! I don't want you to hate me for the rest of my life."

"I don't hate you." She spun and her head kept going long after she was sure her body had stilled. "My whole problem has been that I don't hate you quite enough."

Christian raised his hand to her cheek and she wanted to wince and pull away, but her body was no longer following the rules her brain was sending out.

"Let's just walk." He held out his hand to her.

Victoria contemplated his offer for a moment, but considering it was getting harder to stand still she accepted his hand.

He interlaced his fingers with hers and they began to walk toward the stairs that would descend down to the atrium.

While he had drank away his afternoon and danced with the woman by his side, day had given to night.

"What do you say we walk outside?"

He could see her trepidation. "I don't know…"

"Please." He was going with the fact that fate must have stepped in and given him this night. After all, how perfect was it that someone took the kids and that man who'd pawed and kissed her all day was called away, too. Yeah, fate was giving him one shot to show her how much he'd missed her.

They walked through the front door of the hotel and he kept her hand in his. As of yet, she hadn't shaken hers loose.

Desperately he hoped that the booze, now sloshing in his stomach and swimming through his head, didn't make him do anything stupid. God forbid it made him sick to his stomach or make him say things that would make her run.

"Clare said Sonia picked up the kids."

Tori nodded nervously. "They'll stay with her tonight. She was giving me the evening to have some adult fun."

She'd said the words and he felt her tense. Her lips tightened, but she didn't retract any part of her statement.

Christian was extremely happy that Scott had left, now for more than one reason.

"The kids looked cute today. I had no idea they would be in the wedding."

She'd smiled when he mentioned the kids. "Darcy didn't call until late yesterday. They were thrilled to do it."

"You're doing a good job with them."

The smile on her lips disappeared. "It's gotten a little easier now that we have a routine, but I don't know what I would have done if I hadn't had Sonia. The kids needed a lot of adjustment after the accident and there I was always in a cast or something." A tear rolled from her eye. "Sam doesn't remember his parents much, or isn't old enough to really ask, but Ali…" she sucked in a sob that must have stolen her breath, "she misses them."

The tear had become a full on cry and Christian stopped walking and turned to her. "I'm so sorry."

Tori wiped her cheeks with the back of her hand. "I've taken her to counselors and they say it's normal, but it's so unfair. I don't know how to make it better when I miss my sister so much I can't sleep at night."

Christian had never been one who could offer comfort in a desperate situation. He clearly remembered when his mother had cancer, he had sulked around as if he were a victim while his father and older brother kept the family together. And, since he was admitting things to himself, probably because he was more than a little inebriated, the past two years with his injuries and then the accident, he'd been playing the victim again. And again, he was being taken care of all the time.

"Let's keep walking," he offered trying to think of a different conversation that wouldn't steer them back to the accident, though that seemed to be the common ground they now had.

He didn't take her hand, though he wanted to. She had crossed her arms over her chest and walked guarded next to him.

"So, Ed has me overseeing the building of a baseball stadium."

"Really, that's great."

"Not anything like major league, but a small community one."

"See, you can use your talents off the field."

He nodded. He hated it, but she was right. "What about you? How's the team?"

Tori stopped walking and he turned to her. "Do you even talk to anyone from the team anymore?"

He shook his head. He'd had to bury that dream, the one of now managing or coaching, when he buried his best friend and her sister.

"I've been working at a dental office answering phones part time for almost a year."

"You're not doing the physical therapy?"

She turned her arms over, noting the many scars that covered them. Though it was dark he knew what she was looking at.

"How much strength do you have after the accident? Can you do what you trained your whole life for?"

He shook his head.

"Did you forget how many lives changed that night or are you still focused on what you lost?"

She turned to walk back toward the hotel. Christian caught up with her quickly. The buzz he'd had was starting to diminish.

When he caught up to her he reached for her arm and stopped her. "Listen. I'm sorry. I know I've been an ass. I've spent a lot of time thinking about everything I did to push you away and…"

"You shoved me away, Chris. You told me you couldn't marry me and be a father right now so it was over. Don't take away how eloquently you said it." She set her jaw.

He closed his eyes and tried to grasp for the last of the decency he must have as a person. He shook his head and let out a long regretful breath. "I'm sorry."

Tori clasped her hands in front of her and held them there. "I need to go in and get my things. I'll get a cab, but I should go home."

"Please don't. Just stay for a bit and I'll see that you get home safe. I've been looking forward to seeing you since I learned you'd be here. And in my true fashion I seem to have messed up all my opportunities to show you that I can be a decent person."

He waited for her to give him some reaction, but she didn't, so he continued. "Just one night? One night to at least try to mend our friendship?"

Tori's eyes shifted up as if she were looking toward the sky for guidance. Eventually she nodded and he was grateful for that, because he seriously had thought perhaps she'd throw one of her shoes at his head first.

A moment later he felt the unmistakable rumbling in his stomach and realized he'd never eaten anything at the wedding reception.

"What do you say we go back in for some food? Compliments of my brother."

She actually chuckled and he took it as a positive sign. Perhaps he wouldn't walk away from this evening as big a loser as he'd thought he would when he saw her kissing Scott in the parking lot earlier.

"I could really use some grown up food. Currently Sam will only eat chicken nuggets and Ali wants peanut butter and jelly cut into butterfly shapes."

He narrowed his eyes in the dark. "How do you do that?"

"I have a cutter. I've acquired many interesting things since I became their guardian."

He imagined she had.

As they climbed the stairs toward the reception—each of them slowly with limps and creaking body parts—they noticed the guests passing by them heading out of the hotel.

When they reached the top of the stairs they caught a glimpse of Ed carrying Darcy toward the elevator bank, no doubt heading to the honeymoon suite.

Clara met them near the entrance to the room. "Where have you been? Warner gave the toast. You missed the cake and…" She stopped as if she'd only then noticed he was standing next to Tori. "Sorry. I see that you were being social."

"Is there anything I can do to help clean up?" Tori offered.

"The best reason to have one of these things at a hotel like this. We get to walk away when it's all over. The staff is getting a luggage cart right now for all the gifts and Ed and Darcy just headed upstairs."

"What about food? Is there any food left?" Christian was looking around his sister trying to see.

His mother walked through the door. "Go make you each a plate and then find somewhere to eat it. There is plenty of food left and they're just going to throw it all away."

Christian nodded, took Tori's hand, and headed into the room as his mother and sister watched.

The guests had eaten much more than his mother must have thought because there wasn't much left at all.

Tyler walked up next to him with a bottle of champagne and two empty flutes. "Here this one is open so you might as well drink it. They're charging it to them anyway."

Christian managed the bottle, glasses, and his plate.

"Oh, and one more thing." Tyler took a card out of his pocket and placed it into the front pocket of Christian's tux pants. "Room 430. I'm going to head out again and you shouldn't be driving anywhere tonight so you take my room."

Tyler rested his hand on Christian's shoulder as though it were in lieu of a hug, then he turned and left the room.

Christian turned to see Tori walking toward him with a full plate. "You didn't eat either?"

"Like I said I need a real meal. What's with the champagne?"

"Left overs I guess. What else do we have to do tonight but to finish getting drunk and eat free food?"

She laughed and they walked toward a dark corner where there was a smaller table. He figured no one would see them there or worry that they were in the way of cleaning up. They only needed enough time to eat their food and drink their champagne before Tori loaded herself into a cab and drove away from him, again.

It surprised Victoria very much that she was enjoying her evening. Those kisses shared with Scott had almost—*almost*—been erased from her memory.

Christian, though growing drunker with every glass of champagne they toasted with—as she was as well—had become much funnier as they talked and shoved thick slices of ham in their mouths.

"I really suck at this construction stuff," he said slurring his words and leaning in toward her.

"Nah. I'll bet you're great." She tried to focus on him.

He shook his head. "I don't understand it. Really. I'm going to have to find something else to do." He rubbed his hand over his face, which made hers itch. "I'm not good at anything."

Suddenly she could think of many things he'd been good at. And though she didn't want to share them with him, nor did she think they'd earn him a living, they did make her body heat rise. She licked her lips trying to restore moisture to her mouth.

Christian picked up the bottle to refill their glasses to only manage a few drops into each of their glasses. "Ooops. I think we drank the whole thing."

"I see that." They clinked their glasses together and then she was sure she could hear her cell phone chiming.

The noise caused them to both look up and look around the room. It was empty. His family hadn't even said goodbye. They'd left them alone to have their little party in the corner. But where had she put her stuff?

They both stood, slowly and wobbly, and followed the sound of her cell phone alerting her that she had a slew of text messages.

By the main door they found a chair with his tux jacket draped over it, her purse, another bottle of champagne, and a fifty dollar bill with a torn piece of paper attached that read *Don't let her drive. Get a cab. Dad.*

She watched Chris tuck it into his pocket as she pulled her cell phone from her purse.

She scrolled through the messages.

"Is everything okay?" Christian asked moving closer to her.

"Uh-huh." She was able to mumble as she looked at the many messages from Scott.

He wanted her to call him, but she didn't want to. Doing that would alter the moment. It would take her out of this tiny little fantasy she was having and force her back to reality—where Christian wasn't a willing participant.

She simply texted back WILL CALL TOMORROW. GOOD NIGHT. Then she slid the phone back into her purse.

She'd nearly had a moment of clarity to ask for the fifty dollars so she could go ask for a cab when Christian was before her, his mouth on hers, his hands pulling her to him, and her spinning head pushing aside all common sense.

One of his hands slid over her bottom and the other skimmed her back until it was at the base of her neck. Fighting the whirling sensation buzzing through her, she wrapped her arms around Christian's neck and tucked her fingers into his hair.

She wasn't sure how long they'd kissed—how long his hands had roamed her body—how long she'd gone without breathing properly. All she knew was nothing, sober or drunk, ever made her feel as alive as Christian Keller's touches and kisses.

"I need to get a cab," she mumbled against his lips.

"Stay. Stay with me."

She shook her head as he brushed kisses over her temple. "I can't go home with you. I…"

He produced a card key from his pocket. "Here." He pulled back just far enough to look her in the eyes. "One night. Just one night with me. Please."

That sentence said so many things, did he even know that? He wanted to keep her alone, in a hotel. There wasn't an invitation to his home. Had he planned this all along? And he'd been very specific with the one night thing. It was just like him. Promise her forever, take it all back, and then want only one night.

His mouth was back on hers and she couldn't think anymore. No, he couldn't have one night. He couldn't have any, but when his hand grazed her back again, she felt defenseless against herself. She wanted him. She loved him. He wanted her for one more night. Couldn't she give him that?"

"You planned this?" Her voice was weak.

"Tyler gave it to me."

Okay, she'd give him the spontaneity.

Victoria pulled away from his lips and his body. She picked up her purse and walked out of the banquet hall. In her head she repeated the phrase *you only live once.*

She could hear Chris scrambling behind her. As she walked down the hall toward the elevator banks she heard the door push open.

"Where are you going?"

"I don't know," she called back. "Which room?"

Christian stood there. His feet seemed to melt into the ground. Was she kidding? He'd planned to wallow in his own sorrows by drowning them and then staying in bed all week. He didn't anticipate this.

Finally his body caught up with his brain and he followed her to the elevator.

She'd already pushed the up button and was waiting for him.

Christian stood next to her, not touching her, but looking up at the numbers on the elevator. "Are you sure about this?"

"Chris," she said without looking at him. "One thing that differs between you and me is when I commit to something I don't back away. You asked me to stay—one night." Finally she turned to him. "I want to stay."

The elevator door opened.

They walked inside and he pushed the number four. More than once he tried to replay the conversation with Tyler about what room, but he was sure he remembered that part.

Between them nothing was said. They didn't touch. They didn't even look at each other. But an energy resonated between them that anyone around them would surely feel.

When the elevator stopped they stepped out and she followed him to the room he was sure Tyler had mentioned. At least he hoped it was the right room. At that moment, the millions of bubbles within that champagne he'd already drunk were swimming in his head. He eyeballed the bottle in his hand. He wondered if either of them would even want to drink it.

Christian pulled the key from his pocket and Tori took it from him. "I'll get it."

She slipped the key into the lock and the light turned green. She pushed open the door, took a step in, and turned back to him.

He stood there just looking at her. The most beautiful woman he'd ever known was in his hotel room and was all his for the night. He absolutely didn't see this coming when he reluctantly put on his tuxedo that morning.

"One night?"

"One night," he promised again knowing that it was all he could offer.

She nodded slowly then grabbed hold of his shirt and pulled him through the door shutting it behind them, allowing them to forget the world beyond the door.

Chapter Eight

Stillness encompassed the room. A small sliver of light crept through the dark curtains to tell Victoria that morning had broken.

A throbbing in her head reminded her of the night she'd taken part of. The drinking, the kissing, the love making.

Christian's arm was draped over her and his soft breath was warm on her neck. She closed her eyes and breathed it all in, knowing that she needed to get out of that bed and get home as fast as she could. Nothing good was going to come from what she'd done. He'd asked for only one night and she was foolish enough to give it to him. Now she had to pick up where she'd left off when he approached her on that veranda. She had to pick up the kids and pretend that she hadn't done the most foolish thing—sleep with Christian Keller.

The thought was only a memory when Christian's lips pressed to her neck and his body to hers. The sign that parts of him had awakened before the rest of him was pressed into her back. His hands grazed over her naked skin. It was very obvious that one night was going to lead into one more time the next morning.

"I'm glad you stayed," he whispered in her ear.

"Christian," she started to speak, but he lifted his finger to her lips and rolled her onto her back.

"I want you to stay in my arms all morning."

What is he doing, she wondered as he lowered his lips to hers and she accepted him, again. Her fingers pressed into his back. His body moved against hers. Her heart took a tumble and she knew she'd never recover.

When the moment was over, Christian rested heavy against her. His breath unsteady and his heartbeat rapid against her chest.

She had to admit that she had longed to hear the words she hadn't heard from him in nearly a year. In her heart she loved him and would always love him, but she wanted confirmation that she wasn't just a fling that had fallen into a trap.

But the moment of opportunity was gone when her cell phone rang. Christian rolled away and she reached for the nightstand and picked up her phone. It was Sonia.

"Tori, are you okay?" Her voice was bordering on frantic.

"Yes," she said softly.

"It's noon. Where are you?"

Victoria sat up quickly and the night's binge smashed her brain into a million painful knots.

"I'm still at the hotel. I stayed. I'll be there as quick as I can."

"I'd let them stay, but the kids have a birthday…"

"I said I'd be right there." She ended the call.

Victoria pulled away the sheets and stood.

"Is everything okay?" Christian sat up.

"I have to go. Where is my bra?" She began a frantic search.

Christian stood and looked around, finding her bra on his side of the bed. He held it up. "Let me get ready and I'll give you a ride."

"No. No ride. I need to get to my house and get my car. I can't have any distractions. I need a cab. I need to call for a cab."

Christian looked out the window. "There are cabs out front. But let me give you a ride."

She had to weigh it in her head. She really couldn't afford a cab and he did have a car. But as bad as her head throbbed, his had to be just as bad.

"I don't want to owe you anything. I have to get the kids. Remember, the kids that are a burden? I don't want them to be your burden."

Christian watched her gather her clothes and run to the bathroom, slamming the door behind her.

He swallowed hard. He didn't feel like that—anymore. Sure the kids were a burden. All kids were, in their own way, but he didn't hold it against her. He never should have in the first place.

Tunneling his fingers through his thick hair, he let out a long breath. Those words had caused a tear in his future that he never could have imagined. One brief and stupid moment when the pain was too much from both the accident and the end of his career and he didn't think before he spoke.

Christian looked for his pants and pulled them on. He could hear her in the bathroom and she was crying. He'd made her cry. Not this morning or last night, but nearly a year ago.

He hated the selfishness he felt in his heart. After the accident, she had to go through surgeries and intense physical therapy. She had to bury her sister and her brother-in-law and take guardianship of her niece and nephew. It had worked out that she'd moved into their house. That, he was sure, was more a benefit for the kids than for her.

Sonia had been there for her since her own parents had died. Victoria had been alone to deal with everything, because Christian had been having a pity party for years—the accident only had solidified it.

The scar on his forehead began to itch again. He rubbed it—cursed it.

He found his shirt and gathered up all of the remaining items they'd brought with them, though they hadn't had much more than themselves.

When the door opened to the bathroom, Tori stood there as lovely to him as she had been the night before. Though her hair was unbrushed and her makeup was smudged, she was still radiant to him.

He wanted to compliment her, but he was sure she wouldn't take it as such.

She reached for her purse and took it from him. "I've decided to let you give me a ride home, if you're sober enough."

"My head hurts, but I'm sober." He took a step toward her and she took a step back. He didn't like that. "I can take you to get the kids too."

She shook her head. "No. Just a ride home please."

With that she walked to the door, opened it, and headed to the elevator.

Victoria sat in Christian's car with her fingers tightly laced together. She didn't want to talk to him. She didn't want to look at him, because she knew if she did either, she'd begin to cry like a blubbering idiot.

As soon as Christian turned onto her street she began to dig her keys out of her purse.

He pulled up in front of her house. "I'm glad you came to the wedding."

"It was a very nice wedding." She opened the door and he reached for her hand.

"I had a really nice time." She didn't respond. She didn't know how. "How about dinner?"

"You said one night, Chris. One night." There were the tears and she wasn't going to hold them back. Not this time. "I gave you one night." But really she knew he'd given her one.

"I didn't mean it like that."

"I never know what you mean." She sucked in a breath. "Listen, I have to get to Sonia's. I have to get the kids. I have to call Scott." She diverted her eyes when she said it because she didn't really care at that moment about calling Scott. What would she even say? *Thanks for all the nice things you said to me and for going to the wedding, but I went to bed with my ex, but you'll be fine with that right?*

She shook off the thought and decided it wasn't necessary to be nasty to Christian. After all, she did love him, even if she wouldn't tell him that.

"I had a nice evening, Chris. Thank you for the ride."

She climbed from the car, shut the door, and ran up the front steps of the house. From behind her, she could hear his car door open.

Quickly she put the keys into the door, pushed it open, and shut it just as quickly. He couldn't come in. There was a great necessity in him driving away. Standing behind the door with her back pushed up against it, she waited. A few moments later she heard his car drive away.

The tears fell freely now. How could she have turned him away? For nearly a year she'd waited to have him back. There hadn't been a day that she hadn't.

Then, as if a bolt of clarity struck her, she moved away from the door. The kids. She needed to get the kids. There were responsibilities and she'd completely blown them off for a night with Christian—one more night.

Victoria raced up the stairs to her bathroom, where one look in the mirror clearly stated what she'd done all night. Her hair was a mess and her makeup smudged. And the dress Christian's family had bought her still hung on her the second day.

She picked up her hairbrush and quickly ran it through her hair, pulling it back and capturing it into a band for a ponytail, high on her head. Scrubbing her face and brushing her teeth made her feel a little bit more human, but no less rushed. It wasn't until she'd stripped off the dress and pulled on a pair of yoga pants and her old worn out university T-shirt that she realized the car seats were in Scott's car.

She fell to her bed and sobbed before finding her cell phone and calling Sonia.

"Where are you? You're scaring me," Sonia answered the phone, her voice shaky.

"I got home and realized Scott has the kids' car seats in his car."

"And where is Scott? Didn't he stay with you?"

Victoria swallowed hard. "No. He got called away on business. I don't know where his car is."

"Craig can take the kids. I'll bring yours home and we are going to talk. Get a pot of coffee ready. I want to know what is going on with you."

Victoria wanted to argue, but she knew better. She agreed, hung up the phone, and quickly got into the shower so Sonia had less ammunition to fire with when she saw her.

Forty-five minutes later Victoria poured Sonia a cup of coffee and set it on the table as the kids settled in front of the TV to watch Brave for the millionth time. She'd already zipped up Ali's Merida dress, as that was the uniform for when the movie was on.

She sat down at the table and looked up at her best friend whose face already wore the look begging her to spill about her night.

Victoria took a sip of coffee and set the mug back on the table. "Scott had to fly out yesterday. One of his clients got into some trouble."

"And you stayed at the wedding?"

She nodded. "Those people were supposed to be family to me. They invited me, bought my dress, and I wanted to be with them."

"Them?"

"Yes, them."

Sonia sat back in the high backed wooden chair and crossed her arms over her chest. "Christian?"

She cleared her throat. "He was there."

"And?"

Her mouth was growing dry. "And he asked me to dance after we had a few glasses of champagne." She thought a moment. "Or ten."

"So you got drunk at Ed's wedding and danced with your ex?"

"Yep."

"And common sense had you staying at the hotel?"

Or lack of, she thought. "Mmm-hmmm." She sipped her coffee again.

"You stayed the night with Christian at the hotel." Sonia's eyes had grown wider and so had her knowing smile.

"Don't be like that. I was drunk."

"And he took advantage of you?"

Victoria thought about the night and how she'd given into him so completely and how comfortable it had been.

"Not exactly."

Sonia leaned in over the table. "Tori, you're still in love with him. What were you doing?"

"Having one more moment," she said softly.

"And Christian?"

One more night.

Victoria stood up and paced the floor. "I made a mistake. I just miss him so much."

"And did you tell him that?"

"No. I know this is too much for him."

"A year ago it was too much. Maybe now…"

"No." She shook her head and sat back down as to not draw the kids' attention. "Scott seems very interested in starting something serious. He's good with the kids. He can provide for all of us. Nothing that has happened before this weekend bothers him. Christian is still too wounded—emotionally."

"So are you."

That was certainly the truth. Not a day went by that she didn't think about the accident, the kids, the house, her sister, and of course Christian.

"I have too many people counting on me and I'm just going to forget about last night. Thank you for taking the kids and for bringing them back."

Sonia nodded. "I left the seats on the porch. We have multiple sets. Use them until Scott gets back." She stood and waited until Victoria did the same. Then she pulled her into a hug. "It's okay to want him and to love him. Maybe he needs this."

"I can't feel that kind of pain again."

Sonia kissed her on the cheek and said goodbye to the kids. As she let herself out, Victoria sat back down at the table and cried. She already missed him so much it hurt. She didn't want that anymore.

Chapter Nine

Christian had returned home, showered, shaved, and dressed. His head was pounding, but he was on a mission. The evening with Tori hadn't ended the way he'd wanted it to. Whatever he'd said a year ago was still keeping them apart. He needed to remedy that.

As he gathered his phone off the table and shoved his keys into his pocket there was a knock on the door. Wouldn't that be wonderful if that was Tori?

But there was a grand disappointment when he opened the door and saw his sister and her husband standing on his porch.

"I want details," Clara said, pushing past him and into the house.

Warner followed his wife into the house with a reluctant grin on his face.

Christian shook his head and shut the door. He'd love to tell his sister that he had plans, but he knew better. If she wanted something she was going to get it—even if he planned not to tell her. She had a gift. She'd read him.

She was already making coffee.

Christian walked into the kitchen. "Make yourself at home."

"I am. Warner, do you want cream?" Clara asked as she pulled mugs from the cupboard.

"No. I'm fine."

He'd exchanged a look with Christian letting him know that she'd dragged him along and he'd rather be anywhere else.

"So," she started her interrogation. "Do I have my future sister-in-law back? You did keep her at the hotel."

"How do you know that?"

She settled her eyes on him. "I'm not stupid."

"Okay, we stayed at the hotel together. Neither of us was sober enough to drive home."

She was tapping on the coffee maker as if it would brew the coffee faster. "Tell me you worked things out."

"Clara, it's been a year. You just don't have one night and things are back together." Though if his sister would leave his house he could head over to Tori's house and work on getting her back. They'd had one hell of a night and he missed her more than he thought he had.

He understood that a relationship with Tori would never be easy. It had taken him a year to realize that it certainly wasn't easy for her. But if he loved her as much as he thought he did, he could accept the fate she'd been given.

Clara poured each of them a cup of coffee and brought it to the table, where she sat down next to his brother-in-law. "So you *did* have a night." The corner of her mouth lifted in a half smile.

"Are you just looking for gossip?"

"Not really. I'm looking for proof that you're going to move beyond this funk you've been in all year."

"Lovely, thanks." His comment was as snarky as he felt. He sipped his coffee and then set the mug back on the table and looked at his sister. "Listen, I know I was an ass. It has been pointed out to me that I'm the one who ruined the relationship we had. After last night, I want to try and fix that."

Clara's grin was a full one now. "Really? You're going after her?"

"If she'll have me." He pursed his lips. "Of course when I dropped her off this morning she jumped out of the car and ran into the house as fast as she could. It didn't seem promising. Somewhere between all the...between falling asleep last night and her getting a call to pick up the kids this morning her attitude changed."

"You broke a woman's heart. It'll take some work to fix it."

"I know that." He considered his sister for a moment. "I guess I do have one thing on my side."

"What's that?"

"I'm a Keller. Everything eventually works out for the Kellers."

She shook her head. "C'mon, Warner. Our work here is done. He's cocky again."

Christian laughed realizing cocky was more his style.

Victoria spent the afternoon cleaning house. Things were better when she was cleaning—or at least her mind had something else to think about.

The kids had their lunch and settled down for a nap. Even with the dishwasher purring in the background and the washing machine spinning in the other room, the house was too quiet. She'd dusted every room, mopped the kitchen floor and was now scrubbing the toilet.

Her hair hung in her eyes and she blew it away just as the doorbell rang. Victoria stood up, her back aching and her head matching the pain from the night before. With a glance in the mirror she figured she couldn't look much worse and whoever was on the other side of that door was going to get an eyeful. She could care less that her attire was an old pair of Chris's sweats that she'd stolen years ago and her T-shirt had a huge hole near the hem.

With the toilet brush in her yellow gloved hand, she pulled open the door to find a casually dressed Christian standing at her door with a grocery store bouquet of flowers.

Her mouth fell open as she stared at this man in his jeans and well fitted T-shirt. He pushed his Ray-Ban sunglasses atop his head leaving a tunnel in his beautifully dark hair.

"Chris!" She blinked and then blew another hair from her eyes. "Why are you here?"

"I wanted to see you."

"Now?"

He smiled that smile that accentuated his dimpled cheeks and showcased his perfectly straight, white teeth. "What's wrong with now?"

She looked down at herself and then back up at him, but he was still smiling. "I'm busy."

"Any woman in the world would welcome a man at the door over scrubbing a toilet in stolen sweat pants."

She set her jaw. "Really, Chris, I don't think…"

"Don't think." He stepped inside the door forcing her to take a step back and let him in—uninvited. "It's quiet. Are the kids gone?"

"Napping."

"Good." He'd moved in closer to her and wrapped his arm around her waist. Suddenly she was pressed up against him, her arms pushed out to the side to keep her gloved hands and the toilet brush at bay. "I missed you."

"Chris, let me go."

"I want to kiss you."

She tried to steady her breath. She wanted to kiss him too, but under no circumstance was she going to. Finally, forgetting the gloves and any chemicals they might have on them—or anything else she might have touched—she pushed him back.

"Why are you here?" she demanded.

His face had lost that charming smile and now there was worry in his eyes. "I don't want last night to be just one night. I didn't mean that."

"You said it."

"I say a lot of things I don't mean."

That took the wind out of her sails, but started a fire in her belly.

Victoria turned and walked toward the kitchen. She tore off the gloves with a snap as he followed her. She dropped the gloves in the sink and the toilet brush in the trash can so that it wouldn't touch anything. Opening the cabinet above the refrigerator, she pulled down a vase and filled it with water.

Turning around she set the vase on the table and tore the bouquet out of Chris's hands. "Thanks for these," she said as she shoved the bouquet, wrapper and all, into the vase.

She watched his jaw move and the scar above his eye deepened as if it were an angry dimple. "Let me show you how my mother taught me to do that."

He stepped up to her and took the bouquet out of the water. He didn't step away. Instead, he stood right next to her, his body heat resonating off of him and clinging to her sweaty T-shirt. In order to keep her calm she stepped away and walked to the cabinet which housed a cup with scissors in it, high enough to not be touched by little fingers.

Holding them as she'd been taught in preschool, she handed him the handles while the pointed tips remained in her clasped hand.

Keeping her distance, she watched as Chris skillfully rearranged the bouquet until it looked perfect. He'd always had a knack for such things.

"Those are pretty," a small voice said behind her and it caused Chris to stop what he was doing and look at Ali standing there, her eyes still sleepy.

"Hello, Ali. Do you remember me?" he asked.

Ali's face contorted as she thought. "You were in the wedding too."

He nodded, but her answer wasn't the one she knew he'd been looking for.

"We've met before. You were younger, but let's see..." He considered for a moment and then looked back at her with a smile. "Aunt Tori and I bought you a pink guitar for your birthday one year."

Her eyes grew big. "I remember you. You played baseball with my daddy."

Christian smiled now, but she saw his eyes had gone moist at her answer.

Victoria nodded. "Yes he did. Look what he brought us." She pointed to the flowers and noticed Christian shift a glance her way as she belittled his gift.

He composed his expression and took a daisy from the bouquet. He cut the stem so it had only a quarter of the length. Moving past Victoria, he knelt down in front of Ali, who still wore her Merida dress. "May I put this one in your hair?"

She nodded adamantly and he tucked the flower in her hair, resting the stem behind her little ear.

"Me too?" Another little voice, this one sleepy, said.

Christian turned and his eyes smiled before his mouth did. Victoria wondered if he knew that.

He looked at Sam. "You want a flower?"

Sam nodded.

"One flower coming up."

Christian pulled another daisy from the bouquet, but Sam protested. "Not dat one. Dat one." He pointed to a decorative stick accenting the bouquet.

Victoria covered her mouth to conceal the smile.

"You got it!" Christian pulled it from the other flowers and looked at it with its many small branches. Then he looked at Sam. "Do you want it in your hair? Or do you want a wand like Harry Potter?"

His eyes grew wide. "Potter!"

"A Harry Potter wand it is." Christian cut off a few of the extra pieces and gave him the straightest piece. Sam laughed and pointed it at his sister. "Dabra!" He shouted and Ali giggled as she ran out of the room with Sam chasing behind her.

Victoria bit down on her lip. "You didn't turn into dust when they touched you."

"That's not fair, Tori. I've always loved these kids. They're my godchildren, remember?"

How could she forget, but somewhere she had.

"You can't just come back into my life you know."

"I know you have a lot on your plate."

"I'm also dating Scott." She hadn't really thought about saying that, but she did. Well, it was true. What was he going to do with that?

He nodded slowly. "Right," he said rubbing his fingertips over his scar. "And you told him about last night?"

She felt that fire he'd lit in her stomach explode. Her fists balled at her side. "Don't go there."

"Can't help it. I wasn't alone when I woke up this morning."

She had so much to say to him, but the tears burning in her throat were choking her. As she opened her mouth to speak, her cell phone chimed a text. She cringed as the message displayed on the lock screen and Christian looked down.

"Boarding a plane. Will be home in time for dinner. Can I see you?" He read the text slowly and aloud so she could feel each pinprick against her skin as he emphasized each word.

Quickly she picked up the phone and held it tightly in her hand. "You'd better go."

"Right. You'll want to change out of my clothes before the man of your dreams shows up." He turned and walked to the front door, opening it, and walking away.

Chapter Ten

Scott's car pulled up to the curb and Victoria watched from the window of her bedroom as he climbed out—and he had a bouquet of roses.

She looked at the flowers Christian had brought her earlier which now sat on her dresser. There was a ball of regret in the pit of her stomach. And the regret was that she had overreacted to Christian. Wasn't he trying, in his own weak way, to tell her he was sorry for what he'd done?

The doorbell chimed and Victoria realized she'd been staring at the flowers. She hurried down the stairs as the kids ran toward the door, too.

"Who is it?" Ali asked.

"Scott."

"Cott!" Sam cheered, the wand that Chris had made him was still gripped in his hand.

Victoria pulled open the door to the handsome man who held the bouquet of roses in front of him.

"More flowers!" Ali said enthusiastically.

Victoria bit down on her bottom lip hoping Scott hadn't focused on what she'd said. He stepped through the door and knelt down on one knee. "Ali, these are for you." Victoria watched as he took a smaller bouquet of roses and handed them to her. Her eyes grew wide and she smiled up at her aunt, who gave her a nod to remind her to say thank you.

"Thank you, Scott."

"You're very welcome."

Sam moved in closer and watched as Scott reached into his front pocket and pulled out a little car—a Lexus that matched his. He handed it to Sam, who then dropped the makeshift wizard wand in the floor.

"Cool!" He shouted as he ran toward the family room with his new treasure. His sister followed with her own bouquet of roses.

Scott stood up and grinned at Victoria. "And these are for you." He stepped closer to her and pressed a kiss to her lips.

Victoria felt her breath catch in her lungs. It was a different feeling than when Christian kissed her. Oh, she'd been kissing too many people. She tried to relax against him, but that ball of regret that had settled in her stomach earlier now grew. Her only problem was she didn't know which man she regretted.

He was still pressed up against her, the roses pressed between them, and he gazed into her eyes. "I missed you."

"You haven't been gone that long."

"I know. I had to see you again. I have to fly back out tomorrow, but I wanted to be with you."

Tears threatened to fall. What had she done? This man was never going to accept what she did with Christian last night. She couldn't tell him she'd made an error in judgment. That wasn't a way to start a relationship.

Well, it was one time and it was just that—an error in judgment. And she and Scott weren't really dating—yet—or were they?

She took the roses and held them to her chest. "Thank you for these. They are beautiful."

"They pale in comparison to you."

That did something funny to her chest. It made it tighten. She gave him a smile and turned toward the kitchen.

"I wasn't sure what you liked to eat, so I didn't start anything yet."

Scott followed her. "I thought I'd take you out to dinner. All of you."

"You want to take us to dinner?" She gave him a quizzical look. "Three-year-olds are picky."

"I like pizza."

The smile was now genuine on her lips. "I know a few kids who like pizza, too."

She turned and opened the cabinet above the refrigerator for a vase, only to quickly remember she'd put Christian's flowers in the only vase she had. She shut the door and fast. From another cabinet she took out a pitcher, filled it with water, and set the roses inside.

"I'll arrange them later."

"I like the pitcher. Do you need a vase? I know I have a few at my place."

She swallowed hard. "I have one somewhere," she said quickly, before anyone else heard and told her where the vase actually was. "Let me get their stuff together."

She hurried to gather the items they would need for an hour outing.

"Oh, and don't let me forget to get my seats from your car."

His nose crinkled up. "Yeah. I'm sorry I forgot them. That's some of why I came back tonight, too. I knew you'd need them. I probably made your day harder. I'm so sorry."

She stood there staring at him. Maybe he *was* Mister Right. A man who took responsibility and said he was sorry was a keeper, right?

They ate pizza and played video games on quarters Scott had gathered from the coin collection in his car. He'd pulled over at a park and pushed the kids on the swings and caught them as they went down the slide. And as if the night hadn't turned into the most fun night of their lives—he took them all out for ice cream. Somewhere, he'd admitted to never seeing the movie Brave, so Sam and Ali insisted that he watch it with them. Ali donned her Merida dress and wig and Sam curled up on Scott's lap, but was quickly asleep.

When the movie was over, Scott helped her tuck in both kids, pick up the miscellaneous toys which had been haphazardly strewn through the house, *and* he stayed to watch a rerun of NCIS.

"Whose you're favorite on the show?" he asked her as she rested against him on the couch, her feet tucked up under her and her face on his chest.

"Gibbs."

"Really? I figured you'd be a Tony DiNozzo kind of woman."

She sighed, "Why do you say that?"

He absentmindedly played with the strands of hair over her shoulder. "I don't know. He reminds me of Christian."

"Christian?"

"Sure the good-looking, athletic type that is always in search of something."

She had to agree, though she'd never thought of him quite like that. "You know that Christian and I have long gone our separate ways."

"I know. I'm not the jealous type, even if he did keep falling over himself at the wedding."

If he had, she hadn't noticed—mostly because she felt as though she'd been the one falling all over herself. But with his comment, she wondered if he knew about them staying at the hotel. Surely he'd say so—or he wouldn't be there.

When the episode was over, Scott gave her a squeeze with his arm around her shoulders and stood. "I should be heading home. I have to go back for the rest of the week so we know all the details."

"Wasn't it just a DUI?"

"So much more. I just can't talk about it."

She nodded. "Right."

Scott gathered her in his arms and pulled her close. "I'll call you. And maybe next week we can take the kids to a movie." He brushed a strand of hair behind her ear. "When they are more comfortable around me, maybe it won't be so weird when they wake up and I'm here."

She inhaled sharply at that as his mouth came down on hers in a warm and passionate kiss.

The next week passed and, just as Scott had promised, they'd taken the kids to a movie.

And it had been another week that she dreamed about the night she'd spent wrapped in Christian's arms.

Scott's kisses were nice, but they weren't Christian's.

His words were sweet, but they didn't make her heart race.

Every day that passed, she wondered why she'd walked away so angrily after they'd spent that one night together after the wedding. What would it have hurt to give him an opportunity to prove that he'd changed? He could have. When he'd said those hurtful things to her, both of their lives had been turned upside down.

Scott wrapped his arm around her shoulder as they walked down the street with the kids before them. Ali on her bike and Sam on his tricycle. "Are you okay?"

"Me? Yeah. I'm fine."

"You look a million miles away."

She tried to compose her face so he'd believe her. "Guess my mind was wandering."

As they turned the corner she saw a posted ad on a bus stop.

THE WRIGHTS—New Album!

Pride swelled in her chest. Clara and Warner sure had made a name for themselves. She was so proud of her. She wondered if she was in town and perhaps they could have lunch. When she got home she was going to call her. She really missed her.

But then, again, reality took hold.

Clara was Christian's sister. She couldn't just be the sister-in-law Victoria pretended, in her head, that she was. But she and Clara were close, why should that stop? After all, she was one of the women to buy her the dress for the wedding—which had turned Christian's head.

"You know I was a little giddy when I got to meet Clara Wright," Scott said pulling her out of her trance. "At the wedding." He nodded toward the bus stop to acknowledge he'd seen the ad.

"Clara? Why?"

"I really enjoy their music and to think you knew her when."

Victoria smiled. That's right. She knew her when.

She thought about the night she met Clara—the night she met Christian. It was a benefit for his Aunt Simone's charity. She'd been Christian's blind date. Nothing in her life had been the same since that night.

"I heard they're going to be opening for someone at Bridgestone. Think we can get tickets?"

That brought a wide grin to her lips. "I'll tell you what. I'll call Clara and ask."

"Really? You don't seem like the kind to use your friends." He nudged her jokingly.

"She loves to be used like that. Besides, I miss her."

"Just because you don't date her brother doesn't mean you can't be friends."

Victoria considered him. He was so perfect, why didn't she feel the same way around him as she did around Christian?

"It wouldn't bother you if I saw Clara?"

"No. You're content in your life. Why would I worry about that?"

Because I'm a big fat liar, she thought as they turned the next corner and headed home.

Chapter Eleven

Office doors were supposed to offer privacy, but when you worked with your brother that wasn't the case. Ed nearly flew through the door in one of his raw, angry moods. He walked right up to Christian's desk and threw down a new razor and a pack of unopened blades.

"What the hell? You think you can barge in?"

Ed plopped himself down in a chair in front of his desk and kicked his feet up on Christian's desk.

"You look like shit. You haven't shaved in almost three weeks. You don't look like you slept either."

"And this bothers you?"

"Yes. You're an embarrassment to the company."

"And that's what you're worried about?"

Ed dropped his feet and leaned his arms on the desk. This was more brotherly, Christian thought.

"No. I'm worried about you. I know this is all about Tori."

He wanted to argue with him. He wanted to stand up and punch him in the jaw, but Ed was right.

Christian sunk into his chair. "I thought I had her back. I thought that night we spent together was going to mend everything and just like that," he snapped his fingers, "I'd have her back."

"So what didn't work?"

"My big mouth. I guess when I asked her up to the room I specifically asked her for *just one night.*"

"And you left it at that?"

"No. I went to her house. I took flowers. Then reminded me she was dating that guy and I reminded her she'd slept with me."

"Real smooth."

He stood up from behind his desk. "I know. Listen, I'm not good at this. And I drove by last weekend and his car was there, again. I'm done. What else can I do?"

Ed stood. "Shave." He turned and walked to the door. "Clara will be up here in a few hours."

Christian shrugged at him. "Why?"

"She's meeting Victoria for lunch. She figures she'll have plenty of things to say to you when she's done."

Ed walked out of the office and shut the door. Well, wasn't that perfect? His sister could still be part of Tori's life, but he couldn't? That didn't even seem fair.

He picked up the razor and looked at it. His brother-in-law Warner would know where they were going for lunch. Suddenly, he was getting hungry.

Lunchtime on Music Row was an eclectic mix of music professionals and tourists trying to catch a peek. It was a good thing Warner told Christian right where to go. Bella Napoli was a hidden gem, but a good one.

He'd heard his sister's laughter before he even saw her. Her back was to him and her lunch date was obscured by the waiter.

Christian walked slowly toward them, not sure of what he wanted to say when he got to them.

The waiter moved just as he neared them, and it was the first time he'd looked at Victoria in almost three weeks.

Something was wrong and she looked sick.

A million things ran through his mind. She had a cold. The kids had been up all night. She was dying.

Her hair had lost that luster it always had whether styled or drawn up. There were dark circles around her eyes and he was sure she'd lost ten pounds in the past few weeks.

The moment she looked up at him he forced a cunning smile, one he used when playing ball and the fans beckoned him to be photographed with them. Her eyes grew wide and that forced his sister to turn.

"What are you doing here? Oh and good, you shaved."

He kept his smile, but he didn't like his sister's reaction.

She stood and hugged him, rubbing his bare cheek. "A goatee? I like it. I really like it," Clara said.

He shifted his glance back to Tori, who looked up at him and smiled. "Hello, Chris."

"Hi." He was suddenly at a loss for all the words he wanted to share with her.

Clara looked around. "Let's get you a chair. We just ordered coffee and dessert."

Good, they were almost done. "Oh, I don't know. I was just walking by and…"

"You're welcome to join us," Tori said softly.

"If you're sure. I'd like that."

Clara waved toward the waiter to bring another chair, but Christian kept his eyes focused on Tori. He was worried about her and it shook him to his core.

The waiter brought a chair and then returned with a plate of Tiramisu just as Clara's phone buzzed on the table.

She picked it up, crinkled up her nose, looked at the dessert, and then set her napkin on the table.

"I have to go. Warner just texted and said they have our interview set up early and want to get started. I have to head back to the offices."

"Good thing you're on the right street," Christian said giving her a wink knowing Warner had texted her on his behalf. He owed him now.

"Chris, pick up the tab, will ya. Don't make my guest pay."

"Oh, no. That's…"

"I got it," he shut down Tori's protest.

Clara gave them a nod and moved to hug Tori who stood. "Take care of yourself."

"I will. Thank you for the talk."

Clara smiled. "I'm here for you." She kissed her on the cheek and walked past Christian slapping him on the back of the head.

He rubbed the sting and took the now vacant chair.

"I guess sisterly hugs are overrated," he said. He was happy that Tori was smiling.

She sat back down and picked up her fork. "How did you set that up?"

"What's that?" He asked picking up his fork and slicing off a bite of the dessert.

"Having Warner page her so she'd leave just as you walked in."

He let the lady fingers melt against his tongue then swallowed hard. "You know me pretty well."

"I guess I do."

He noticed that brought a little bit of a spark to her eyes, which looked hollow. She put down her fork and sipped her water.

"You're not done with this are you?" He asked taking another forkful of the dessert.

"I'm fairly full already." He watched as she took her napkin and wiped her brow.

"Are you feeling okay?"

She sipped her water again. "Yes. I think I'm catching something."

He took another bite and then cleared his throat. "Is Scott around? Is he taking care of you?"

She shook her head as if she wasn't bothered by his question. "He's been busy and out of town a lot. I'm fine. I might have Sonia hold on to the kids for me so I can rest tomorrow."

It was instinctive as he reached his hand across the table and rested it atop of hers. "If you need help I'm always a phone call away. I can even watch the kids."

Her eyes widened and he knew what she was thinking— and he was tired of her thinking it.

"I'm sorry I ever told you I wasn't ready to be someone's dad. But I can handle kids for a few hours to give you a break. Okay?"

She considered him before nodding.

"Okay, well you call me if I can help."

"I will."

They made small talk until the waiter brought the bill and Christian paid it, as his sister had insisted.

He walked her out to her car and opened the door. "Thank you for lunch. Tell your sister I had a nice time and thank her for the passes into the concert."

He grinned. "Were you using my sister?"

"Not at all." Her cheeks blushed. It gave her a nice glow which made her look better than the pale sickly color she'd had in the restaurant.

When she'd climbed into her car and put the keys in the ignition he'd considered bending down to kiss her. The feeling was nearly overwhelming. Instead, he closed the door, stood back, and watched her drive away.

~*~

Victoria sat at Sonia's kitchen table as the sound of children's laughter enveloped her.

"What are they doing?"

"Playing dress up." Sonia handed her a glass of sweet tea and sat down across from her. "How was your lunch?"

"It was wonderful. I miss Clara."

"And how is Chris?"

Victoria narrowed her glare on her best friend. "Why do you ask?"

"C'mon. If he knew you were with his sister he'd make an appearance."

She felt her cheeks heat and by the smile that formed on Sonia's lips she knew it showed.

"He stopped by. Clara made him buy lunch as she was *called out* for an appointment."

"Set up by Chris?"

She nodded and then blew out a breath when her stomach suddenly didn't feel so well.

"You okay?"

"I just don't feel well."

"You haven't felt well in weeks. The kids seem fine."

She nodded. "I think I'm just worn out and going to that wedding made me get all worked up. I haven't slept a full night since."

"You can take a nap here if you'd like."

She shook her head. "I'll be fine."

Sonia laughed at her. "You act like I did when I was pregnant with the kids. Well, come to think about it I feel that way now too. I'm just always exhausted."

"I guess I didn't get the nine months for each of them to acclimate. I was just thrown into all-nighters with a crying girl who misses her mommy and daddy and a little boy who is an escape artist and shows up at my beside."

Sonia laughed again. "You did block the stairs with that gate I gave you, right?"

"Of course."

"Good."

She visited with Sonia for a while longer before getting the kids ready and heading home for another night of Brave and the requested chicken nuggets. But Sam had promised that if he had chicken nuggets he'd also eat some broccoli. She hoped he was a man of his word.

Luckily, Victoria had been reprieved of having to eat the nuggets when Scott showed up with Chinese food.

"You're a saint," she said as she put a piece of pork in her mouth.

"You were looking too skinny. You need substance."

She laughed, but she knew she'd lost some weight since she couldn't seem to eat much. Perhaps she had PMS, though she usually gained five pounds and wasn't so sick.

Victoria sipped her water from the bottle which Scott had brought with the dinner. In her head she was making a mental calculation and working on a mental calendar. When was her last period? They'd been wonky since the accident with all the medications and surgeries, but she couldn't even remember the last time she'd had one.

A wave of nausea moved through her body. She stood and ran to the bathroom up the stairs in her bedroom. Quickly she turned on the sink, noticing that the handle was leaking a bit, but that was a problem for another day.

Her face was perspiring, her stomach lurched, and her brain was fully engaged in a conversation she'd blown off from earlier in the day. *You act like I did when I was pregnant with the kids.*

No. No. No.

She did more calculations in her head as her body temperature cooled as she pressed water to her face from her fingertips.

It had been three weeks since Ed and Darcy's wedding. Three weeks since...

Now her stomach moved and she lifted the toilet lid and let go of all the dinner she'd just eaten

"Victoria, are you okay?"

She could hear Scott call to her, but couldn't call back as another wave took over.

When she looked up he was standing in the doorway. Quickly he grabbed for the towel on the rod and wet it under the running water.

He handed it to her and then took her hair and held it back for her.

"Oh, Scott. Go. You don't want to see me like this."

"Honey, this is fine. You're sick. You need some help."

Why couldn't she just fall head over heels in love with this man? He was so perfect in every way.

When she felt her stomach settle she reached up and flushed the toilet and with Scott's help got to her feet.

"C'mon. Let's get you into bed."

She shook her head. "The kids."

"I'll get them put to bed. I'll get dinner cleaned up too. Then," he brushed a strand of hair from her face, "I'll make myself a bed on the couch. I'll only be a few feet away if you need me."

There was a protest on her tongue, but she couldn't manage it. Every time she'd had surgery, Sonia had stayed at the house. This was the first time she was really sick and she needed help.

"Thank you," she whispered.

Quickly, exhaustion took over her body. At some point she knew she'd heard the kids in the hallway with Scott on their way to bed, but she slept through the night.

She'd nearly forgotten he was there until the next morning when she walked downstairs to make her coffee. The deep breathing from the living room startled her a moment. Then she saw him splayed out under a Mickey Mouse blanket. Her breath hitched in her throat at the sight of his bare chest.

Steadying herself with a cleansing breath she walked toward the kitchen.

She was more than grateful that she'd brushed her teeth before coming down, because when Scott walked into the kitchen and pressed himself up behind her she'd let out a sigh. His hard body was close against her and his lips were on her neck.

"Are you feeling better?"

"Uh-huh," was all she could manage.

"I can call in sick and *take care of you*." His voice had dipped sensually and she swallowed hard.

"I have to work."

He let out a groan and then gave her a peck on the cheek. "Maybe tonight and the rest of the weekend."

He moved away from her and headed down the hall to the bathroom and Victoria let out the breath she'd been holding. Right. It was Friday. He could come back and spend all weekend.

Scott would be spending the night.

Dear Lord, was she ready for this. She looked down at her shaky hand. Yes. She was ready.

Chapter Twelve

There was a lot to be done before she picked up the kids from daycare. If Scott was spending the night, it was one more mouth to feed. She needed to make a plan and squeeze in a trip to the grocery store.

As she walked into the store, the scents accosted her nose and made her stomach roll. Oh, this wasn't going to be a good thing. She needed some anti-nausea medicine.

When she made it to the aisle with the medicine, it wasn't hard to realize there were many reasons for such medicine. Looking down, she saw the pregnancy tests all lined up. There was every kind of test. Easy to read. Spell it out for you. Boxes with multiple sticks.

Her stomach rolled again.

No. She wasn't pregnant. She had the flu. She was the guardian of two young children. She just had the flu.

As she moved past them something made her stop. Well, what would it hurt to at least know for sure—even though she was *sure*.

An hour later she was home and the kids were getting settled. She'd hung up Ali's new art work on the refrigerator and given Sam a few Cheerios to hold him until dinner.

She took the bag of groceries and began to unpack them, putting away each piece. When she got to the pregnancy test, she just stared at it as if she'd forgotten she'd bought it.

Her nerves twisted inside of her. She looked up and the kids were building something with the old toilet paper tubes they'd decorated one day. It would only take three minutes. She had three minutes.

Quickly, she took the box up to her bathroom and shut the door.

It would be quick and painless and it would be over. Then she could go on with her life.

She read the instructions, more than once, and then took the test.

As soon as she was done she set the test on the top of the toilet and went to wash her hands. But the faucet this time nearly came off in her hand. With water spewing all over she reached under the sink and turned off the water source.

She let out a sigh and grabbed towels to sop up the mess just as she heard a crash and a cry from down the stairs.

Without hesitation she ran down the stairs.

"What was that?" She turned the corner to see that Sam was holding his hand over his forehead and all around him were scattered cars.

She scooped him up. "Are you okay?"

He nodded with a tear dangling from his long, dark lashes.

She looked at Ali. "What happened?"

"He was stacking cars up high and he stood on the Lego bucket to get higher on the shelf and it fell over."

Assessing the room she could now see the big pre-school Lego set all over the floor with all his cars. But he seemed fine.

In the midst of the commotion the doorbell rang and she set Sam on the floor and ran for the door. There stood Scott in his lawyer-man suit looking very handsome and in his hand he carried a bag. She tried to steady herself when she realized it was the bag he'd have packed all his things in to stay the night.

He stepped into the house and pressed a kiss to her lips. "This was one of the longest days of my life."

"Why?" She gulped back.

"I couldn't wait to get to you."

The moment was quickly over taken by Sam tugging on Scott's leg. "Car tower!" And then he ran back.

"He wants you to see it."

Scott nodded with a smile as he set his bag by the stairs and followed him.

It was comfortable having Scott around as she started dinner and he played with the kids. He was a good role model and so good with them.

Dinner wasn't fancy. Spaghetti and meatballs, but she'd made some garlic bread to appease the adults at the table.

After dinner it was time for a movie, which she and the kids sat and did every Friday night. Scott was right along for the ride, having changed out of his suit and into a pair of sweat pants and a T-shirt which accentuated his very nice biceps. It was then she noticed he had a tattoo peeking out from under the sleeve. She hadn't noticed that when they'd gone swimming or even this morning when he was pressed up behind her.

"What is this?" She reached over and pushed up the sleeve.

He smiled shyly. "Tribute."

The tattoo was very small, but it was a set of angel wings and the word mom.

She had to swallow back tears. The Kellers had a tattoo. Clara had hers on her wrist. The infinity symbol and the word family.

Victoria had lost her entire family. Her mother had died of cancer years ago and her father a few years later from complications with diabetes. Then her sister died in that horrible accident. She'd been alone for years and now here was this man…

She reached up and placed her hand on his cheek, drawing him closer for a kiss.

"What was that for?"

"I really like you. I'm glad you're here."

There was a tingling in her body now and the movie they were watching couldn't end fast enough. When it did she announced bed time and they didn't even have to pick up their toys first. That at least made the walk up the stairs quicker.

She and Scott tucked in each of the kids, kissed them good night, and then headed for the bedroom.

The moment they both were in the room Victoria shut the door and turned the lock. This was it. She was moving on!

"What happened in here?" Scott asked as he turned toward the bathroom. "Oh, you had a leak. I can…"

He'd stopped talking just as she realized she hadn't been back upstairs since she'd taken that test.

She hurried to the door and saw him holding the pregnancy test in his hand.

Her heart pounded hard in her chest and her head spun. She couldn't read him. His face had gone pale and blank.

She watched as his Adam's apple bobbed in his throat as he swallowed hard and then looked up at her.

"You're pregnant?"

"I am?" That wasn't really the response she'd meant to give.

"Is this yours?"

She licked her lips to moisten them as she thought of an answer. But she simply nodded.

"You're pregnant and you didn't tell me?"

"I bought the test on a whim. Something Sonia said the other day about me being sick…so I bought it. I took the test and forgot…"

"You're pregnant?"

Victoria dropped her shoulders. "I guess I am."

Scott ran his hand over his chin and she could hear the scratching of his stubble against his palm.

"This puts us in a very awkward situation. You and I haven't had sex."

Tears were stinging her eyes and she tried to bat them away.

She watched as Scott considered. "How far along do you think you are?"

Victoria balled her fists to her side to keep her hands from shaking. "About four weeks."

The color in his face began to deepen. The darkness in his eyes did the same.

He lowered his head and looked at the stick again before looking back up at her. "The wedding?"

She nodded.

"We've been dating since then."

She nodded again and now the tears streamed down her face.

Scott pursed his lips and she noticed there were tears in his eyes too. "Do I even have to ask whose baby this is?"

"Scott, I didn't mean…it just…no," she finally resigned and hung her head.

Scott shook his head and took a long deep breath before walking toward her. She lifted her head and he handed her the pregnancy test which boldly had printed on it PREGNANT.

"Here. You're going to want to show this to the responsible party."

He walked past her and unlocked the bedroom door.

Victoria turned and followed as he pulled open the door and headed down the stairs.

"Scott, I'm so sorry. You have no idea…"

"Save it. You're going to need to keep your strength for your baby and the kids. Tell them I said goodbye."

"Goodbye?"

He picked up his bag which still sat by the stairs. "Victoria, I don't mind taking on the responsibility of others. I thought making a life with you and the kids would be fine. And under different circumstances I'd never have given another thought about taking on this baby, too. But knowing that commitment doesn't mean anything to you and that this baby was conceived while we were together…well that's a game changer. I don't take to people who lie to me."

He opened the door and walked away.

Chapter Thirteen

Victoria fell to the floor still gripping the pregnancy test in her hand. How could she have gotten pregnant? How could they not have even considered it?

She didn't even bother to wipe at the tears that fell down her face.

How could her life have turned into such a disaster?

But that didn't feel right? That wasn't the right assessment of her life. She had lost a lot. That part was true, but she'd never ever give up on Sam and Ali. No, her life had just changed.

She ran her hand over her belly. And now there was this.

Lifting her hand to her lips she began to sob harder. There never had been a doubt in her mind that she'd carry Christian's baby—if she had a baby at all. But this wasn't the way she wanted to do it—alone.

What if he turned the baby away just as he had turned her and the kids away?

Her breathing eased when she thought about the Kellers and her tears began to dry. Christian might push her aside, but they wouldn't. They took family very seriously. Again, she ran her hand over her stomach. Her baby would be okay. He or she would have a family that would help to take care of them.

She let out a breath. For now she'd wait it out and see what happened. After a doctor appointment to confirm, she'd decide how she would handle it. Chris was going to have to be told.

But for now, this was her secret. Even if she couldn't have Christian, she'd have a part of him.

With that thought she forced herself up off the floor and back to her bedroom where she faced the mess of towels under the sink. Tomorrow she would call Clara and see if her Uncle John might have some time to look at it.

Under the circumstances, she was sure Scott wasn't an option and she didn't want to ask Christian. She wasn't ready to see him—and, to be honest, he wasn't too handy.

~*~

When Christian heard the front door slam he headed toward it to see who had just barged into his house. It wasn't much of a surprise to find his sister standing there. He shook his head. When would he ever get privacy? First his brother busts through his office door and now his sister has done the same in his house.

"Now what?" He dropped his shoulders. It had been a long night and he didn't want to be social.

"Are you any good at plumbing?"

He actually snorted a laugh. "Are you kidding me?"

"Really. I need a faucet fixed."

"Then you call Uncle John, not me."

Clara followed him back to the kitchen and stopped, resting her hands on the back of one of the chairs.

"It's not for me. Tori just texted me and said she needed Uncle John to come fix her sink. I figured you should go."

"I don't think so." He walked over to the dishwasher he'd been unloading and continued to pull out warm, clean dishes.

"C'mon. Even if you can't fix it, it'll get you in the house."

"She has company."

"Oh." She pulled out the chair and sat down, which wasn't what he wanted. He wanted her to go.

"If she needs something fixed she should ask Mr. Lexus to either get his nice manicure messed up or hire someone to do it."

"How do you know he's there?"

Christian set his jaw. "Because for two nights I've driven by," he swallowed hard. "Multiple times."

"You're spying?"

"No. Just driving by." He turned away from her and whispered, "At all times of the night."

"You are spying."

He turned back to her. "What does it matter? His car was at her house all night Thursday and was still there this morning when I went to work. And then last night at dinner time and at nine o'clock it was still there. I've been replaced." Again he turned around. "And I don't blame her."

"I really thought after the wedding and lunch…"

"You thought wrong."

She nodded and stood. "I'll call Uncle John."

"Good."

"Chris, I'm sorry."

He shrugged. "I did this to myself. But the good news is I have a date tonight. So I'm not going to worry or think about Tori. She seems to be happy and she's moved on." *Rather quickly after our night together.* "She doesn't need me crashing anymore lunch dates."

~*~

It was just past one when Victoria answered the door to the handsome "Uncle John."

"You got my message," she said grinning as she pulled open the door.

"Honey, I'd fix anything you needed. I'm glad you thought of me. Retirement has me bored off my ass."

She laughed. "I doubt that. I've seen what you've done to the theater in the past few years."

"My wife and her projects."

Victoria missed going to see productions at the theater John and his wife Arianna owned. She remembered seeing Clara there when she played *Annie* when she was little. She never would have thought then that she'd know that girl who had mesmerized her so much. And to think., she was a big country star now.

"So which sink is it?" John asked walking into the house with his tool box.

"The bathroom in my bedroom." She pointed him up the stairs.

John began walking up the steps. "Where are the kids?"

"Napping."

"I'll be super quiet."

She smiled hoping he might do just that.

When they walked into the bathroom he looked the sink over. "This shouldn't take too long, but the tube to the shut off doesn't look too good either. I'll put a new one there too."

"Thank you. Whatever you need to do I'm fine with. I'd rather stop the problem before it costs me so much more."

"Smart girl." He set his tool box down and looked up at her. "Are you feeling alright? You have dark circles under your eyes."

Victoria kept a smile pressed on her lips. "I'm doing fine. Just a little something that's going around I guess."

He nodded at her. "You need rest."

"You're probably right."

"Why isn't that man of yours fixing this? Really, it's not a tough job."

The smile left and tears threatened. "Let's just say, there isn't a man right now. You're it I'm afraid."

"Well, sorry to hear things didn't work out. But whenever you need me you just call."

"I will. Thank you."

"I'll get to this. I'll let you know if I need anything."

Victoria walked out of the room as John got under the sink and began working on the tubing. She could hear all sorts of noise downstairs, but what she didn't know was that he'd kicked over the trash can in the bathroom and found the pregnancy test she'd thrown there.

Chapter Fourteen

For the first time in weeks, Christian had a spring in his step. A new pair of jeans and a trendy new shirt, which made him look bad ass—at least that's what he thought of it when he looked in the mirror. He'd dug out his old Rolex and even had on some *sexy* boxers—just in case. There was a woman out there that didn't just want to let him in to push him away and he was going to take advantage of a nice evening with her. And, if she was willing, maybe breakfast too. He was tired of being the stand-up kind of guy. It hadn't been working for him.

He picked up his keys, checked his wallet for necessities, and headed out the door ready to take his mind off—everything.

He started his car, found some good ole Hank Jr. on the XM Radio, and put the car in reverse.

A moment later he was damn glad that it was a newer car and had one of those backup systems to it, because the thing began to beep and scream at him, forcing him to slam on his brakes before he hit his Aunt's car, which had just shown up behind him.

Christian slammed the car in park and jumped out to make sure he hadn't actually hit her.

"Are you okay? Is everything okay?" He began his bombardment the moment Arianna stepped out of the car. "God, why did you pull up on me like that?"

"I need to talk to you." She was out of breath and it was scaring him.

"Mom and Dad are okay right?"

She nodded. "I need to know if you've talked to Tori."

His heart began racing uncomfortably and his stomach did some kind of dead-man's flop. "No. Tell me she's okay.

There wasn't some accident or anything was there? The kids? The kids are okay?" He couldn't catch his breath fast enough to ask more questions.

Arianna put her hands on his shoulders to calm him. "She's fine. Kiddo, she's fine."

He nodded and began sucking in as much air as he could.

"Listen, John went over to fix her sink. I just wondered if you've talked to her recently."

He thought about the day he'd interrupted her lunch, but that'd been it. Besides that he'd just been a stalker-like creep and driven by her house to see Scott's car parked there all night long.

"No." He backed away from his aunt's grasp and motioned to the car. "If she's okay then I'm glad. I have a date with a red-head who seems to have been asking about me since the wedding. So if you don't mind…"

"She broke up with that guy—I think."

"You came over here to tell me that?" He shook his head. "She has made it very clear that she doesn't want anything to do with me. I made a mistake once in the darkest time of my life and she's made a point to remind me of that."

"I think she could use your friendship right now."

"I don't want to show up there and say *sorry you got dumped.* I want to move on."

He turned around and climbed back in his car, but his aunt stood there with her arms crossed over her chest.

"I'm telling you she needs someone right now."

"How do you know this? Did she cry to John? Did she cry to you or Clara?"

She shook her head. "No. Just—will you go to her?"

"No." He looked up at his aunt one more time. "I'm late. Will you please move your…"

"She's pregnant."

He was sure he could still hear the cars warning sound going off, but in fact it was the blood rushing through his head and his ears. He swallowed hard.

"She told you that?"

Arianna shook her head. "No, but John wouldn't just gossip."

"She told him that?"

Again Arianna shook her head and then walked closer to his car. "He found the positive test in the trash in her bathroom. And she's been sick."

He thought of how she looked when he'd seen her at the restaurant.

"Uncle John isn't the kind of guy to get involved in things like this."

"Not unless he cares about someone. You may not be with her, but she was part of our family for a long time. I think it would be a nice gesture if you just went and checked up on her."

"Because the big lawyer who swooped in, to make me look so bad, now looks just as bad. Get her pregnant and then run?"

"Christian…"

"I'm sure she'll be okay. She has Sonia to cry to if she needs to. I have a date." His phone buzzed. "And there she is, wondering where I am."

Arianna stepped back from his car and he shut the door between them. He watched her get back into her car and back out of the driveway. A moment later he watched her drive away down the street.

When she was out of sight he backed out of the driveway too. His date lived east of Nashville.

He turned and went north—toward Tori's house.

The steering wheel was slick under his hands which were moist with perspiration. The buttons on his shirt had become constricting and the car was slower than it should have been.

That Scott guy was a piece of work. How could he do something like that to her? How could he...

Quickly Christian rolled down his window. The air was too thick to breathe.

He realized he'd done nearly the same thing to her when her sister had died. Only there wasn't nine months to get used to the idea of someone coming into your life. No, it was sudden and it was painful. She'd been physically a wreck after the accident, in and out of surgery. The kids had emotional issues that needed to be tended to, as well as her emotional issues. She'd lost what was left of her family that night—and she'd lost him.

He'd been so big on all the bad things happening in his life he pushed her away when she needed him the most—and now this.

As he sped down side streets and through major intersections, he thought about her. What had she been thinking? Why did she get pregnant? As if that was going to solidify Scott staying.

He grew angrier. He wanted to go to the man's office or his house or his country club and punch him right in the jaw. How could he do something like this to Tori?

And then back again—the guilt balled in his stomach.

Who was he to rush in to the rescue? He was a hypocrite.

As he turned down her street he made himself a promise. It would be Tori for the rest of his life or no one at all. He loved those kids and had since the minute each of them was born. There was a commitment to them which he'd promised to Dave. He'd turned his back on them when he turned his back on Tori.

No more. It was fine that she didn't want him in her life as a lover or a husband. She might not even like him enough to be her friend, but it wasn't going to stop him.

If he had to use the kids as leverage, then that's what he would do. He'd made that promise to Dave and Ashley and he was going to see it through.

He swallowed hard. And when Tori's baby was born he'd love the baby too, because it was part of Tori—even if he felt like that just might kill him.

The air was thick, but Victoria wasn't sure if it was because of the heat outside or because she'd sucked in a breath and had forgotten to expel it. The door handle was still clenched in her hand and she stood there staring at Christian all dressed up as if he'd come to take her out.

He'd taken his sunglasses off and slid them to the top of his head. Those dark eyes locked on to hers and then the corner of his mouth turned up and it made the dimple in his cheek crease.

"I know. You weren't expecting me," he said, finally breaking the silence and she realized she hadn't even greeted him.

"Ever." It was curt, but that was what she was feeling toward him.

He nodded tucking his lips between his teeth. "I heard you weren't feeling well and I thought I'd stop by and see if you needed anything."

She narrowed her eyes on him. "Who told you I wasn't feeling good?"

His eyes were darting and it made her wonder what he'd really heard.

"John said you were sick."

She let the tension out of her shoulders. "Yes. Seemed to have a touch of the flu. I'm fine now, but thanks for stopping."

She tried to shut the door, but his foot seemed to wedge it open.

Swinging it back open she held up her hand. "What is it with you? Why are you really here?"

He bit his lip. "Because I also heard that Scott wasn't here anymore."

"So you're here to just take over? I don't need a man in my life. I can't seem to keep them happy enough to want to stay."

"That's not true."

"Chris, I don't know why you're here, but I have baths to give, dinner to make, and a book to read for the umpteenth time. You look like you have plans and perhaps you should just go do whoever you have plans for."

She saw the tension in his jaw and knew that was his sign that he'd be turning around and getting into his car, but he wasn't moving.

Instead, he stood there. His chest heaved enough that she knew he was calming himself with his breath intake. But he hadn't retreated or said anything else.

"Would you mind if I came in so we could talk?" He asked, his voice low and deep.

That had her hand gripping on the doorknob a little tighter.

"You dressed up to come over here?"

His jaw tightened again. "No. I had plans, but I've changed them. Can I come in and talk?"

"Like I said, I'm busy. If you come in you can only stay for a few minutes."

He nodded and as he passed by her, his cologne filling her nose and making her knees weak, he said, "We'll see about that."

Chapter Fifteen

Victoria felt her stomach twitch as he walked by. It was almost as if the baby knew he was there, but she knew that was absolutely impossible. She'd had enough time to Google search pregnancy. What she was feeling now was the mix of emotions that always stirred in her when Christian was around.

She noticed he hadn't stopped walking once he'd made it through the kitchen. He'd walked all the way out to the family room where the kids were making a fort out of blankets and old sheets.

The words to protest him getting down on his knees and rolling up the sleeves on his shirt seemed to lodge in her throat. What was he doing?

It was obvious he had somewhere to go, why was he playing? What made him think that she wanted him in there with them?

But then she heard Sam giggle and that made Ali giggle—and then Chris.

Tears burned her throat. If she told him right now that she was pregnant with his baby, would he scoop her up in his arms and promise to love her forever? She shook her head and turned away from the play going on in the other room. He wasn't the same man she'd fallen in love with years ago. This man was broken.

Whatever his reason for stopping by, the kids seemed to be having fun and she was going to utilize the time.

While Ali convinced Christian to make paper hats for all of them, Victoria switched out a load of laundry and took the basket upstairs.

She set the laundry basket on Ali's bed and opened the dresser drawer. The picture which was prominently displayed on the top caught her eye as it always did. She took a deep breath and picked up the frame.

Her beautiful sister smiled up at her with her loving husband by her side. Each of them held one of their children, who had already grown so much since the picture had been taken.

She ran her finger over the picture and her heart ached. Ashley and Dave would be so proud of their children. And she hoped that if they could see them from heaven that they approved of how she was raising them. She was doing her very best.

"Hey," Chris's soft voice came from the door.

She wiped the tears that were clinging to her lashes. "Hey."

"Ali sent me up for Poppy?"

Victoria let out a chuckle and set the frame back on the dresser. She turned toward the bed draped in pink and picked up the pink plush dog resting on the pillow.

When she turned back, Christian had picked up the frame and was studying it.

"This was only a few months before the accident."

She nodded. "Easter."

Christian closed his eyes. "You wore a yellow dress and carried a basket which Sam filled with eggs."

"Yes," she said on a breath.

He opened his eyes. "It was a happy time."

"It was." She shook the memory from her head and handed the worn dog to him. "This is Poppy."

Christian took him and looked at him. "She's had this dog since she was born."

"Never goes anywhere without it." Victoria wrung her hands. "I'm surprised you remember."

"Don't be. I told you these kids mean something to me. I promised their father that I'd always take care of them when he asked me to be their godfather. I forgot how important some of the promises I made were. I'm having some clarity."

She heard what he was saying, but how truthful was he about it?

He shot her that handsome smile. "I'd better get back down there. Princess Ali has a tea time and Poppy is her guest."

Victoria smiled. "Thank you."

"Truly the most fun I've had in a long time." He turned to walk out of the room.

"Chris," Tori called. He turned back around. "Why are you here? Why are you *really* here?"

He took only one step back into the room and looked down at the well-loved dog. "I made a lot of promises to a lot of people and then I let those promises slide so that I could wallow in my own self-pity. One of those promises was to Dave. You're doing a great job with these kids. But I know once in a while you could use a few minutes to catch your breath."

Those darn tears were back and she batted them away as fast as she could. "I don't expect you to do this all the time."

"You should. I know there isn't any hope for us. I ruined that and I accept responsibility for that. But I'm going to be here from now on. You are a strong woman and you could do this all on your own—and have been. But you don't have to."

"That's a big promise."

"Yeah, well in the long term not so big. They've already grown so much."

She nodded and he took one more step into the room.

"And if you ever need to talk, I'm here. Anything—okay?"

She sent him a curious look, but he didn't go on. She only nodded and forced a smile.

"Back to the fort. If you need help with dinner let me know. I'll leave when their baths are done and you're done reading whatever book you have to read."

"*Red Fish, Blue Fish.*"

His brows came together with a crease dimpling his forehead. "Really? That's the book?"

She nodded with a chuckle. "I have it memorized."

"I have it memorized and haven't read it in thirty years."

He turned and hurried back down the stairs to play in the fort.

Victoria sat on the bed and rested her hand on her stomach. Did he know? How could he?

She let out a long deliberate breath. No matter what he'd just said to her, she wasn't going to tell him—not yet. Christian had made many promises and she needed to know he'd keep a few of them, before she told him her secret. For now, she'd simply enjoy the moment to breathe while laughter resonated from downstairs.

Christian had helped them with the fort. They'd had a tea party and now they were picking it all up, with some protest, to get ready for dinner. Victoria was standing over the stove boiling noodles, he thought, and he took a moment to walk over to her.

He made sure not to touch her. "You don't have to feed me. I dropped in uninvited. I'll catch dinner when I go."

"It's only spaghetti with sauce on the side. Sam doesn't like sauce. But I have plenty."

He smiled. "If you don't mind. I'll bring over some groceries tomorrow to offset some meals."

He noticed she swallowed hard, but she didn't turn to look at him. "You're coming tomorrow?"

"I would like to stop by and maybe I could take the kids to the park for a little bit. I saw a small glove the other day at the store. It's not too early to get Sam playing catch. Or Ali for that matter."

Tori continued to stir the pot of noodles, but her jaw tightened. "You don't just have to suddenly come and step in. They've been this long without a man in their life."

"I don't think they should be without one any longer."

"Chris, I can't let them get used to having someone around to have them just up and leave."

He knew where she was going and he wasn't going to let her win this. "That isn't going to happen. I'm here for the long haul and even if you and Scott get back together I'll be here to help you out. I promised Dave I'd look after them and I will."

Her lips softened. "Scott isn't coming back."

"Well, if someone else comes along then. The point is, I'm here. I never should have *not* been here."

He could see the tear well in her eye, so he turned away and went back to picking up little cars and stuffed animals.

Victoria watched Chris help the kids. Why was he there? This was crazy. And now he wanted to come back tomorrow?

Sure, she felt that warmth she always did when it came to him, but she couldn't have him around knowing that he was just going to break her heart again. How could he not? And now it wasn't just her heart he was going to break, it would be Sam and Ali's too. Luckily Scott had only been around a few times, but Chris—he was different. Ali remembered him. Sam, he didn't remember much, but he'd obviously attached himself to Chris. She toyed with the thought again; about telling him about the baby. If this kept up, there'd be no choice.

She watched as he carried both of them, one on his back, the other on his waist—which had to hurt like hell—to the bathroom to wash their hands for dinner.

Give yourself some time, she warned herself. *He's probably not even going to show up tomorrow.*

Dinner was pleasant. Chris refused to let her serve him until the kids were sure they had enough food. When she did serve him, he was gracious. Not that she'd expected anything less. His mother had raised him right.

After dinner he offered to clean up while she got their baths going, and he'd made it clear he'd like to be there for the reading of *Red Fish, Blue Fish.* She agreed and, a half hour later, she called down the stairs for him.

She sat on the edge of Sam's bed, ready to read the book. The moment caught her in the chest when he walked into the room in the dim light. It was too cozy.

This was how it was supposed to have been. She wasn't going to cry. This crying was getting out of control, but having been around her sister and Sonia when they were pregnant, she knew it was part of the process.

He stood near the door and leaned up against the wall casually. With a nod he gave her a wink to start the story.

Victoria moistened her lips with her tongue as they seemed to have gone dry.

Ali clutched Poppy and Sam's eyes were already heavy. She started the story, but even the easy rhymes were hard to follow knowing Christian was standing there watching her with those sexy brown eyes.

By the time she was finished, she realized Christian was the only one still listening. Both Sam and Ali were fast asleep.

She closed the book. "I think you wore them out tonight."

"Trust me, I was fighting it myself. They wore me out too. I don't know how you do this every day."

A part of her wanted to tell him that, with him there, the night had been much easier.

She looked down at the little blonde angel clutching the worn out dog. In the past few months, she'd become just too big for her to carry and it had become necessary for her to wake her almost every night to walk to bed.

"I'll get her." Christian moved toward her.

"Are you sure? She's too big for me now."

He nodded and moved in to scoop her up in his arms. Victoria had to press her hand to her stomach as she watched him carry her out of the room. They were a family, whether he'd stay or not. She had that part of him growing inside her and it was up to her to let him in.

She turned off the light and hurried downstairs to compose herself before she had to face Chris and tell him goodbye.

The kitchen was spotless and all traces of dinner had been cleaned up. Even the pot had been washed and leftovers put up.

The hum of the dishwasher caught her attention, but then there was something else. A rattling—no a buzzing of a cell phone on silent.

She looked around until she found the source. Chris's phone had fallen out while he was playing with the kids and it was on the floor in the family room.

Victoria picked it up as it buzzed again. The message splayed on the screen. It was what appeared to be one of seven messages from a Rachael.

DON'T BOTHER TO CALL.

Again, those stupid and pesky tears welled in her eyes. She could only assume Rachael was the woman he was dressed up for. Christian didn't usually just look that good unless he was out to impress.

There was a sharp pain in her chest, but she had to let it go. He wasn't hers to keep. She'd made it as clear to him after they'd spent the night together that she didn't need him—just as he'd made it clear he couldn't make a family with her.

A wave of nausea began to move through her. Not now. Not now! She pressed her hand to her stomach, but it wasn't going to hold.

As she looked up she noticed Christian walking into the kitchen. He moved to her swiftly.

"Are you okay?" His eyes were wide and he looked scared. Why would he be scared if he thought she was only sick? But those were the eyes of someone frightened.

"I don't feel well."

"C'mon, sit down."

He helped her to the couch. "I'll get you some water."

She could hear him in the kitchen opening and closing doors to cabinets. A moment later he was back with water.

"Here sip this."

She reached for the glass, but her hand was shaky. He helped her until she got a sip down and everything began to feel more normal.

"Better?"

She nodded, but now her eyes were growing heavy. "I'm fine. I'll be okay."

"Tori, I can stay. If you still don't feel well I can..."

"No. No, you can't stay."

He only nodded as if that was exactly what he thought she'd say.

"I've managed in worse situations. Besides, Ali will be up in a few hours. You being here will only confuse her."

"A few hours?" His eyebrows narrowed.

"She wakes up a few times a night looking for her mother. Most of the time she doesn't even realize she's doing it."

He shook his head. "That's terrible, for both of you."

Victoria shrugged. "It's just part of our life." She felt the vibration of the phone in her hand again. She looked down at it and she wanted to squeeze it into a million pieces.

She looked up at him and lifted her hand. "This is yours. You left it out here."

"Oh. I hadn't even noticed." He looked at the screen, frowned, and then tucked it into his pocket.

She took another sip of the water and then focused in on him. "Did you stand up a date?"

The lines around his eyes deepened. "I came here and that was more important."

"I don't suppose Rachel thinks so."

He didn't say anything else and she'd wished he'd just tell her that Rachel was his assistant or something, but she knew better. She'd tried to move on with Scott and it was now obvious he'd tried to move on with Rachel.

"Can I help you upstairs?"

She wanted to tell him that if he would tuck her in and tuck himself in next to her that would be the best. But she knew it wouldn't make everything better. Christian had to want that.

"I'll be fine."

He'd tried to convince her again, but she held to what she thought was best. "And you really don't have to come by tomorrow. You're busy."

"I'll be here. Let me be here."

She walked behind him to the door. He pulled it open and turned to her. She was almost waiting for him to try and kiss her. But he didn't.

"Can I bring anything tomorrow?"

Shaking her head she looked into his eyes—those dark and sexy eyes. "No. And like I said, you don't have to come."

"I'll be here," he reiterated through clenched teeth.

He stepped over the threshold.

"Chris," she called and he turned back. "If you can't always be here for them, then please don't be. I can't explain to them your leaving if you do this."

His eyes narrowed. He pursed his lips and walked away.

Chapter Sixteen

It had been a week since Victoria had held that pregnancy test in her hand. A week since Scott walked out of her life and somehow Christian had walked back in.

He'd been there every night after work and, just as he'd promised, he was helping out. On Sunday night he'd walked through the door with groceries and again on Thursday. They'd taken walks around the park as a family. He'd bought that ball and two gloves and begun teaching both kids how to catch.

He wasn't just stepping in as the playmate either. On three of those nights last week, he'd cooked dinner so Victoria could play with the kids. She'd even found him in the laundry room doing their laundry.

She hadn't quite yet figured out his motivation, maybe it would make it easier to finally tell him about the baby since he'd begun to integrate himself into their lives.

On her day off, she'd been able to get an appointment to the doctor and her pregnancy was confirmed. Now she sat at Sonia's kitchen table finally ready to tell her best friend—well, she'd get to it.

"You'd think these kids hadn't seen each other in a month. Gretchen has been waiting all week to show Ali her new Barbie."

"I'm glad they get along so well. I'd like to think they'll stay friends as long as we have."

Sonia nodded and took a sip of her iced tea. "Maybe Gretchen will know when Ali is hiding something from her."

Victoria tightened her lips. She wasn't sure why she hadn't told her yet. She should have known Sonia would know something wasn't right with her.

"Scott and I broke up."

Sonia turned, her mouth open. "Why didn't you tell me that?"

"Probably because the next day Christian started coming around."

Sonia blinked her eyes rapidly. "Why? Did you tell him Scott left you?"

"Not really. I told John when he came to fix the sink. He'd asked why my guy wasn't fixing the sink and I said I had no guy. Then he asked if I was sick and I told him I had been. Then Christian showed up because he heard I was sick and that there wasn't anyone around to help me out."

Sonia narrowed her eyes at her. "So taking Scott to the wedding was really a good thing? I mean it woke Christian up."

In more than one way.

Sonia covered her hand with hers. "This has nothing to do with Christian just showing up, does it?"

Victoria swallowed hard and tried to gather her nerves. She took in a cleansing breath and let it out. "I'm pregnant."

Sonia's eyes opened wide and then her mouth opened and closed. She covered it with her hand and then slowly dropped it. "Oh, Tori."

"That wasn't the reaction I thought you'd have. It was mine, but..."

"How long?"

She ran her tongue over her teeth. "Five weeks."

Sonia covered her mouth again. "Christian's?"

Tori nodded.

"And is that why he's come around?"

Victoria shook her head. "The only other person that knows is Scott."

"And that's why he left?"

She nodded.

"Oh, honey."

"It's going to be okay. I don't expect Christian to hang around much longer. And when he finds out about the baby, he'll run. He's been playing favorite uncle all week, but it's only been a week. If he couldn't be a father to the kids, he can't be father to his baby."

"But you can't do this alone."

"I don't think I'll have to. The baby is a Keller. They won't let me do this alone."

"But is that enough?"

"It's going to have to be."

Sonia stood up and walked around the table and pulled Victoria up out of her chair and pulled her into an embrace.

"I'm here too. Whatever you need. I'm here."

"Thank you," Victoria said pulling back. "But don't say anything. Not yet. I'm not ready for the kids to know or for Chris to know."

"You don't have forever on this. He'll figure this out soon you know."

"I know."

Victoria thought she'd see how the week went and then she could decide how she wanted to handle telling Christian.

~*~

Christian tapped his pencil against the top of his desk as he looked over the plans for the baseball stadium. In the past two weeks, he'd had a change of heart when it came to the project.

He'd been playing catch with Ali and Sam each night when he got to their house. And even at three-years-old,

Sam showed the same promise his father had. Dave should have been major league. Christian would never understand why he hadn't been picked up.

The stadium was now a personal mission to Christian, something he could honor Dave with.

He jotted down notes to take to the next meeting as his office door opened. His brother walked through.

"I have come to the conclusion that there is a no knocking rule when it comes to family entering my office," he said without looking up from what he was doing.

"I figure it saves me the hassle of you telling me to go away." Ed sat down in front of his desk. "How's the stadium going?"

"I think the plans look good. I only have a few suggestions."

"Good. I'm glad to see you are finally looking enthusiastic."

Christian blew off his brother's comment. He realized he hadn't been very gracious about the job or the project.

"So what did you need?" Christian set the pencil down and leaned back in his chair.

"Rachel was asking about you. Well she asked Warner, who asked Clara, who called Darcy, who sent me."

Christian snorted a laugh and picked up his pencil again. "And just what did Rachel want to know?"

"Why you stood her up a couple weeks ago."

"And she's just now sending messengers?"

"Well? Why'd you stand her up? She was trying to get your attention at the wedding and then she finally gets a date and you don't show up?"

"Why do you care?"

"Just isn't like you."

Christian shook his head and dropped the pencil again. "I've been spending my evenings at Tori's with her and the kids."

"No kidding." Ed sat forward and leaned his arms on the desk. "You're back together? I thought that was a one night thing?"

"It was. I'm just helping her out. I promised Dave I'd help take care of those kids and I did a lousy job last year."

"You sure did."

"Thanks." He sat back in his chair.

The evenings he'd been spending with them, and the weekends, had become very special to him. They'd become a family. There was only one missing piece. Tori still hadn't told him about being pregnant.

Christian had come to believe that maybe his Uncle John had been mistaken. She'd been sick and was having a hard time getting over it, but he was sure by now she'd have said something about it. If she hadn't said something he thought the kids would have or even Sonia might have dropped a hint. But there had been nothing.

But every night that he was there to listen to the bedtime story and tuck in the kids, he began longing to do it every night—forever. And if she was pregnant, it was a chance to be there from the beginning of a life—even if it wasn't a life he created. How could Scott walk away from her knowing such a thing? Then again, maybe Scott didn't know and she thought it was better to keep it from him.

His mind spun the situation around a million times. If Scott didn't care and he was the one who stepped in and loved the baby, perhaps he'd make up for the year he'd been an ass—but this time he'd do it for love of the kids, love of the baby, and his undying love of Tori.

"So what are you going to do?" Ed stood and looked down at his brother. "Are you going to try and get her back or are you just going to help her out? You know…I need to pass back something to Rachael."

Christian laughed. "I just now decided that I'm going to ask her to marry me again."

Ed's eyes opened wide. "Are you sure about that? That's going back on everything you told her."

"I was in pain. I was devastated. Let's just say I don't think I was in the right mind set. But, yeah. I'm ready to marry her and be there for the kids. I know I won't replace their father, but I can help them learn who he was. I can bring that part of their life back."

Ed was shaking his head, but smiling. "I think you have come back to us, little brother."

He was ready to be back. The pain, devastation, and self-pity had turned him into someone he not only didn't like, but that he didn't know. It had to be over. The sun was up for another day and he'd better take the time to make the most of it.

All he had to do now was convince Tori that he wanted to be the man in her life—even if she *was* pregnant with the child of another man.

Chapter Seventeen

The phone had rung off the hook all day long. Victoria never thought a dental office could have so many problems, but it just must have been in the air.

The doctor already had four emergency procedures that had come in and Victoria had to reschedule his entire day. Actually what happened was the appointments just had to be tacked on at the end of the day. In other words, she would have to stay. Then, the afternoon receptionist called. Her son fell at school and she was taking him to the emergency room with a broken arm.

Victoria was stuck.

She called Sonia to beg for help, but with Craig on a business trip she had no back up either. Plus, all of her kids had doctor's appointments. It wasn't something she could reschedule very easy.

There was a panicked surge that ran through her body when she called Christian's cell phone.

"Hello?" His voice was hushed when he finally answered. "Tori, is everything okay?"

"I'm fine. Did I catch you at a bad time?"

"I have a moment," he said, but she could hear him moving as though he'd walked out of one room and into another. "What's up?"

"I'm stuck at work until six-thirty. I can't get to the kids and Sonia can't help me out."

"I'll get them." The offer was so quick she almost wondered who she'd really called. She'd expected some sort of argument that he'd do his best, but he couldn't promise, and he'd see what happened in the next few hours…

"Tori, what time do I have to get them?"

"They need to be picked up by four."

"Okay," he drew out the word. "I'll need to stop by your office and get your van to get them in. I'll be to you by three. That should be enough time, right?"

"Yes," she nearly sighed. "Chris, this means the world to me. Thank you."

"I'm here for you and the kids, sweetheart. I'll see you around three." His voice had grown soft again as though someone might be there.

A jealous pang shot through her, but she brushed it away as much as she could. "I'll see you then."

Christian looked down at his watch. He had two hours to convince the planners of the baseball stadium that it needed some changes. If the meeting ran over he'd have to walk out on it and that was going to cause Ed quite a headache. But he wasn't going to go back on a promise he'd made to Tori—not again.

The planners were open minded to his suggestions and the smile on his uncle and his brother's faces were priceless. He'd stepped up to the plate, he'd nearly struck out, but it looked like maybe he'd make a home run with this project after all—and with Tori.

As the meeting wrapped up, he checked his watch for about the thousandth time.

"Do you have a hot date?" Ed said walking around the enormous table in the board room, his uncle following right behind.

"I promised Tori I'd pick the kids up. She's stuck at work."

He saw the exchanged look between his uncle and brother. Each of them had a cocky grin on their face.

"Christian Keller is going to the daycare to pick up the kids. Did you hear that, Zach."

"Don't think I've heard better news in years." He gave Christian a wink and walked out of the room.

"Laugh all you want."

Ed placed his hand on his brother's shoulder. "I'm not laughing. I'm very happy for you."

Christian looked down at the stack of papers he was piling together. "I love her, man."

"You always have. Since the moment you first saw her at that fundraiser."

"What if she won't marry me?"

Ed shrugged. "All you can do is ask and find out, right?"

Yes, that's what he'd do. But he needed to remind himself if she said no, he couldn't just walk away. He still had made a promise to Dave and he'd keep it. She wouldn't get rid of him quickly, but he really hoped she'd say yes.

As he drove to her office, his mind was racing with everything he wanted to do to make a proposal special. He wasn't just going to pop the question. He needed to ease into it. He needed to woo her a little, make her want him back.

It had been a few weeks since he'd been hanging around. Things were comfortable. The kids were comfortable. Maybe tonight when she looked at him with those blue eyes, he'd finally lean in and kiss her goodnight as he walked out the door. And tomorrow night the kiss would be longer.

As he pulled up to the office, he noticed the parking lot was packed. He pulled up behind her van and double parked. If this was how her day was going she'd need something special for tonight.

She had an angry older gentleman at the desk and a phone to her ear when he walked through the door.

"Mr. Peterson, he'll be right with you. I promise it won't be more than ten minutes."

The man grunted and took an empty seat. Christian walked up to the desk and she held up a finger to him. "Yes, he can take you next week. Right. We will call you the night before. Thank you," she said as she hung up the phone. She blew a loose blonde curl from her eyes. "I owe you." She pulled her car keys from the pocket of her scrub top and handed him a twenty. "I'm out of gas too. I just realized that about a half hour ago."

Christian took the keys only. "I got it. Do you want us to come by and pick you up or can you handle the truck?"

Her lips pursed. "I'm a native Tennessee girl. I can drive a truck, Chris."

He winked. "I know. You called the day care. They know I'm coming?"

"Yes. You'll need your ID."

"I got it. And you'll be home about six-thirty?"

"Around there. The house key is on the ring, too."

"We'll be there." He reached across the desk and took her hand, giving it a squeeze. "Anything else I can help you with?"

Her eyes had gone soft now when she looked at him. This was a good sign. "No. I can't thank you enough."

"You don't have to. I'm here for the long term."

He didn't give her a chance to argue. He turned around and walked out to the parking lot to maneuver the vehicles so that his truck was parked for her and he could take the aging minivan to the gas station and then pick up the kids.

A smile formed on his lips. Never in a million years did he think this would be the highlight of his life—but it was.

Victoria could smell him in his truck—feel him. It was more than just his cologne. There was a bottle of water in the cup holder and a Gatorade bottle in the seat next to her. A hard hat and a pair of muddy work boots were on the rubber floor mat behind her seat, no doubt something he used when he was on a site.

The thought interested her. He didn't talk about working for Zach and Ed much. It wasn't what he'd wanted to do with his life, but the accident had landed him there. His baseball career was only a dream now. Even the opportunity he'd once had coaching seemed to have slipped away.

But he did mention that Sam had his father's arm. Maybe someday he could coach Sam—and Ali. Her gut twisted and she set her hand on her stomach. Or even his own son could play ball with him.

It was as if for the first time she noticed the tightness of her stomach. His child grew inside of her and she'd yet to tell him. He'd been so wonderful stepping in and they were really a family, why hadn't she decided it was okay to tell him yet?

Another feeling washed through her as she started up the massive truck. She loved him. Well she knew she always had, but she was in love with this man that had just recently come back into her life—the man who doted on the kids and on her.

The fear that he might turn her away when he learned about the baby was suddenly diminishing.

She had another doctor's appointment in a week and the doctor had said they'd take a peek to see how everything was going. Maybe she'd see if she could get one of those sonogram pictures to give him. If he could see what they'd created together it would be better. Yes, that's what she would do.

Victoria backed out of the parking lot with a renewed sense of purpose. She wanted Christian back, and not just as a promise to the kids. She wanted him back in her life. She wanted him to be the father to his child that he'd want to be.

She expelled a long breath. She wanted him as her husband. Maybe she'd just ask him.

Chapter Eighteen

The house was quiet when Victoria walked through the door. But the smell that filled her nose was delightful. She set her purse on the couch and walked to the kitchen. The oven light was on and there was chicken baking, a salad in a bowl, and rolls cooling on the counter. The sound of laughter came from the back yard.

She looked out the window to see Ali pushing Sam around the yard in the little red car his father had bought him for his first birthday. Tears stung her throat. What would his parents think of how he was turning out?

The moment had drawn her in and she never even heard Christian walk into the kitchen. She didn't even know he was there until he walked up behind her and slid his arms around her.

She jumped, but he didn't let go. He kept his arms around her, as if it was the natural thing to do between them—and once it had been.

She knew it was much too early to feel the baby move, but she swore that the energy that resonated between Chris and her stomach was a connection. It was magic.

He rested his chin on her shoulder. "They are happy, good kids."

"They are."

"You're doing a great job."

"I'll never replace them though—their parents."

"No but we can keep their spirit alive. We both loved them and we can make sure those kids know who they were and how much they loved them."

She turned around in his arms and his hands rested on her waist. It was too intimate to put her arms around his neck, so she held on to the counter. "I don't want to do this without you anymore."

"You don't have to."

"Are you scared?"

"More than you can imagine." He raised his hand and tucked her hair behind her ear. "But that's what it's all about, right? Each day is an adventure and you never know what will happen."

"I can't let you stay around them if at some point you find that it's too much and you want to leave."

He shook his head and his hand rested on her cheek. "Never again. I'll never let you down again." He moved in closer until their bodies were pressed together.

His eyes had gone darker, just like the night she'd stayed with him in the hotel. The fire which ignited under his touch burned through her. Should she tell him about the baby now? Would he accept her silence about it and understand why she waited?

He didn't move in any closer or try to kiss her, but she thought that the look in his eyes said he'd want to.

But then the back door opened and the quick steps of little feet and hard breath had him stepping away.

"Auntie, come see! Come see!"

Both kids hurried to her and took a hand leading her to the back yard.

Out on the back patio was a new planter full of flowers. Every color and kind was represented. "We planted these for you."

"For me?"

"Yes. Me and Sam picked them all out. All but this one." She pointed to a grouping of pink daisies. "Chris picked those out for you."

Victoria swallowed back the tears that stung in her throat. Damn, why did everything make her want to cry lately?

"You did this for me?"

"The kids did." He winked. "We wanted to do something special for you."

"Ya!" Sam added. "You special."

The tears didn't hold back now. She scooped up Sam and held him tightly as Ali hugged her legs. This was her family and that included Christian.

Sam lifted his head from her shoulder and held out his arms. "Cwis! Hug!"

She watched his eyes grow moist too as he moved in to hug their little family. Yes, she knew it was theirs.

Not only had they planted her flowers, but the kids had also helped Christian with dinner. Ali had been in charge of stirring the pudding and Sam had been in charge of sprinkles. He wasn't sure if there was a limit on too many sprinkles, but Tori didn't seem to mind.

"I just set your laundry on your bed," he said. "I didn't want to go through your drawers."

She looked at him with a sweet smile on her lips. "You did my laundry?"

"Yep," he said as he poured more milk into the special cup Sam drank from that didn't spill. "I vacuumed the van too when I got gas. I'll take it to work with me next week and get the oil changed if that's okay with you."

"Sure," she choked out.

He gave her a wink. He could see she was a bit overwhelmed, but he wanted her to know he'd handled it. The kids had been picked up, the van had been gassed and vacuumed, dinner made, laundry done, and even flowers planted. The kids were healthy and happy and he'd done it with a smile on his face. They could do this—if she could just forget about how stupid he'd been.

They had a routine. After dinner they always took a walk. He'd walk next to Tori, but he'd never taken her hand. Until tonight, he'd made sure to stay physically away from her. He didn't want her to think that only the physical was driving him as it had the night of his brother's wedding.

But tonight he had a change in mind. "Let's take a drive."

"A drive? Where?"

"I have something I want to show you guys."

They agreed and as a family they piled into the van. He started the van and they drove. No one questioned where they were going. The air wasn't thick enough that they had to have the air on, so they rolled down the windows and took in the early evening sounds. Twenty minutes later Christian pulled up to the fenced off lot.

"What is this?"

"My office."

Tori narrowed her eyes. "Your office?"

He smiled. "This is the project I'm in charge of. It's a baseball stadium."

"It's dirt!" Sam shouted from the back trying to see, but restrained in his seat.

Christian turned and smiled at him. "It's going to be a baseball stadium. Do you want to go see?"

Sam nodded his head and that was a good enough answer.

They walked around the orange fencing at the mound of dirt. He was sure that was all Tori could see and he had to admit to himself a few months ago that was all he could see too. But now, standing in front of it, he could imagine the parking lot, the stands, the scoreboard, the concessions.

There wasn't anything he couldn't already see. He assumed this was how his brother and uncle saw the world—full of possibilities yet to be built.

Christian took his phone out of his pocket. "Here this is what it will look like." He'd knelt down next to Ali and Sam and pulled up a picture of the drawing. They both looked at it and then out over the dirt.

"I wanna play," Sam looked him directly in the eye.

"You want to play ball."

"On a team. Like daddy."

He saw Tori turn away—obviously to collect herself. Christian cleared his throat. "Well, at your age you start with T-ball. Does that sound good?"

He nodded with excitement. "You be my coach."

Now he was going to have to compose himself. Tori had turned around as if she needed to see his reaction. He noticed her hand had rested on her stomach and that made his head spin.

It was here. It was now. This whole world was spinning around him and he wanted to scoop it all up and keep it just like this.

"You want me to be your coach?"

Sam nodded.

"Okay, then. I'll be your coach. That means I have to keep hanging around, is that okay?"

"Where else would you go?" Ali asked.

That was the final moment he knew he couldn't live his life without them. "Ali, if you'll have me, I'll never go anywhere else again."

"We like having you around and so does Auntie."

Christian shifted his eyes toward Tori who was wiping tears away. "You like having me around?"

"It wasn't my plan to not have you hanging around."

Chris stood and moved toward her. He rested his hands on her hips. "Can you forgive me? I didn't know this was exactly what I wanted."

"Are you sure this is what you want? You can't play ball again, Chris. You won't be in the majors. I have them and I can't take off on a moment's notice and be anywhere you want to be."

"You are where I want to be."

"Is it enough?"

"It always was, I just lost sight of that."

She rested her head on his shoulder and he pulled her in close.

"Chris, I've never stopped loving you," she whispered in his ear and that was when the first tear broke free and ran down his cheek.

He pulled back so that their foreheads touched. "I've been thinking about the plans we had once. You were supposed to have my name by now."

She tucked in her lips and held back her sob. "I know."

"Maybe we could consider making those plans again."

She rested her hand on his cheek and then looked at the children who were collecting rocks from the mud. "I'd like that, but..."

He didn't like that. He didn't want a *but*.

"Let's talk about this next week. I'm very overwhelmed right now and I'm even a little light headed."

"You're still not feeling well?" He wished she would tell him about the baby. It would all be easier if she could just tell him that she was carrying Scott's baby, but if that was the case, she'd probably want to see what Scott's plans were before she included Christian in on it. That was how she worked. He understood that, but it wasn't making things any easier.

"I'm okay."

He was going to seal this. He was going to make sure she knew how he felt.

Christian leaned in and pressed his lips to hers. At first her lips were tight, but as his hands slid around her back they became more pliant. The kiss could have gone on all night, but when he heard Ali's, "Ewwww," he knew it was time to drive back home.

After all, he had a lot of planning to do. He was asked to wait a week before they talked about making plans. That gave him a week to find a new ring—a bigger better ring. He should think about selling—or renting—his house. She'd want to stay in Ashley and David's house for the kids and he would agree with that. And, he let out a long breath, he needed to look into T-Ball leagues. It looked like he was going to coach after all. The majors couldn't hold a candle to the home run he'd just hit.

Chapter Nineteen

The drive home that night had grown quiet. The only noise was Sam babbling about baseball.

Christian's head was a million miles away. There were a lot of plans to make in a week.

They all left their shoes on the front porch and walked into the house—as a family.

"Time for baths," Tori announced and two grumbling kids threw themselves on the couch. "C'mon. We had fun now we have to get our baths."

"Do we have to go to school tomorrow and day care?" Ali was taking each step sluggishly.

"School is fun."

"Nu-uh. Peyton says that I'm dumb since I have Poppy."

Tori shook her head. "I'm sure Peyton has something just a special to her as Poppy is to you. She must really be having a bad day if she makes fun of you. Try to understand, ask her if she's okay. Then if she's still mean you can tell your teacher too."

That seemed to suffice for Ali.

Christian walked behind her up the stairs. "You think that'll work?"

Tori turned and her eyes were angry. "Would you rather me tell her to punch the girl in the nose?"

"No."

"Why do you think kids are mean?" She'd stopped walking and stood a step higher than he was, looking down at him. "It usually starts at home. Peyton might be having issues with her mom. Her dad moved out last year. And if I remember right," she stopped and looked for Ali who had gone into her room, "he left to be with his girlfriend."

Christian nodded. He remembered when his dad left; he too had gotten into some trouble. And a few months later when his mom remarried his dad's best friend, it had gotten worse.

"Imagine what she's going through. She doesn't even know how to talk to anyone. So what does she do? She takes it out on the little girl who doesn't even have a mommy and daddy anymore. This is how they think, Chris. You have to teach them to be the bigger person. Find out what is bothering her and maybe you'll be the friend she needed."

He'd been that kid, that was for sure. It was a teammate who, after punching Christian in the nose for being so mean, asked what was wrong and they had become friends.

"And if she's just a mean girl?"

"Then I guess you punch her. But there is a time frame."

She turned back around and headed up the stairs. Christian followed behind shaking his head—and admiring the view in front of him.

Baths were drawn in separate bathrooms. Ali enjoyed her privacy and Sam still liked to play in the bubble with all of the tub toys he could find.

When Ali was finished Tori came back to help with Sam just as Sam took a bucket of water and dumped it on Chris.

He could see Tori trying not to laugh as she scolded Sam.

"I guess this would be a good reason for me to bring over some clothes," he said and her eyes widened.

"I'll get you a shirt."

She walked out of the bathroom and Christian finished rinsing off Sam and wrapping him in a towel. When she came back she had the old T-shirt she'd been in the day after Ed's wedding. The day after he'd made love to her all night.

Christian ran his hand over the stubble on his chin. "Are you sure you want to part with that?"

The air was thick in the room and Sam must have felt it too. He wiggled out of the towel and ran down the hall, naked to his room.

Christian stood up and looked her in the eyes.

She licked her lips. "How about I lend it to you."

"You're going to lend me my own shirt?"

She nodded slowly. "And maybe you could bring it back with a few other things."

Christian took another step toward her. "That just said a lot."

She lifted a shaky hand and rested it on his chest. "I missed you." Her eyes scanned him and then met his. The blue staring back at him had grown darker. "I don't just mean missed having you around."

To steady himself, he placed his hands on her hips. "Are you sure you know what you're saying? The last time we got into this situation it didn't end so well."

"I didn't think you'd show back up the next day."

He took another step closer, wrapping his arms around her waist. Tori lifted her arms and draped them around his neck.

She wiggled slightly when the wet T-shirt pressed against her. "Maybe you should change now."

"I wouldn't want to get you all hot and bothered when I take off my shirt."

"Chris, when I said wait till next week, it meant a lot of things. I have some things I need to take care of. But, after that," she brushed her forehead against his lips. "Will you move in with us?"

It certainly wasn't what he thought she'd ask, but he couldn't have been happier that she did. If he was in the house and they were a family, there was no way she'd turn down his proposal.

"I would love to do that. Are you sure?"

She pressed her head to his chest. "I'm very sure."

Christian stood there holding her pressed to him. One week. He could live for one week knowing that after that, he'd have unlimited time for hugs, kisses, and love making.

But there was one more thing. Only one thing he needed from her and that part was killing him. He needed to know if John was right about the baby.

He kissed the top of her head. "Tori, is there anything else you want to tell me? Anything you've been keeping from me?"

She didn't look up at him and she was silent for what seemed to him a very long time.

"Just that I love you. I have always loved you."

He rested his cheek on the top of her head. That would have to do, he thought.

~*~

Christian had watched his brother's courting of Darcy from day one. He'd paid attention and he knew that when you wanted to wow a woman you took Aunt Simone, Aunt Regan and your mother to the jewelry store to pick out a ring. Not to leave anyone out, he also invited his sister and his Aunt Arianna, though he was nervous about seeing her. She was the only one who assumed she knew what was going on with Tori.

Perhaps he'd invite her to meet him first. That might make a difference.

The jewelry store was just off Hillsboro Pike. There was a pizzeria around the corner. He'd just see if she wanted to catch a bite and maybe a beer, or two, before they went shopping.

"This isn't a very big table. You can't tell me I'm the only one here to help you pick out a ring, because honey, we're in trouble." She made her accent thick when she spoke.

"No," he laughed and ordered a beer when the waitress came for their order. Arianna followed suite. "Listen, remember what you came to my office to tell me?"

"About Tori?"

"Yeah. She hasn't said anything to me yet."

"That was weeks ago. She hasn't said a word?"

"No." He let out a breath. "I don't know if Uncle John just misread it or..."

"He said it was one of those tests that spelled it out. I don't think he misread it."

"I just can't figure out why she won't tell me, unless she thinks Scott should know first. She asked me to wait till next week, to discuss any future plans. Do you think that if she is pregnant that's what she's doing?"

His aunt bit down on her lip. "Who ever thought someone like Tori would be caught up in something like this?"

"Caught up in what?"

"She moved on from you, got into a relationship, had one night with you, then went back to him, and now she's pregnant."

"It doesn't paint a pretty picture. That's not how she does things."

"I know." She rested her hand on his. "I didn't mean it like that. There has to be a reason, right?"

"Yes. She knows I'm going to ask her to marry me. And if she doesn't, she's really clocked out," he laughed. "Why do I have to wait till next week? None of this makes sense."

"So why do you really have me here early?"

"You can't say anything. You can't even hint at it. I want them to respect Tori."

"There isn't anyone in our family who doesn't." Her voice carried the hint of irritation.

"I know. I know. Promise me that this is only between you and me."

"I promise." She nudged him. "But regardless of this, you're going to ask her to marry you again? This is really what this is all about?"

"We have something—wonderful." The waitress set his beer on the table. He picked it up as she walked away and took a sip. "I don't just mean me and Tori. I mean all of us. It's only been a few weeks, but we really have a family."

"Chris, I'm excited for you." She sat back in her chair and considered him for a moment. "And when she does tell you about the baby how will you handle that…I mean if it is Scott's?"

"*If?* What does that mean?"

Arianna took a sip from her beer and held it in her mouth before swallowing it down hard. "You know for sure it's Scott's?"

"Of course. They were in a relationship…"

"In which you interrupted."

The wind rushed out of his lungs. He hadn't even considered that their one night could have anything to do with her being pregnant. He had totally decided, on his own, that she had just gone back to Scott and that was that. Never once did he consider that this might have been the reason Scott had left in the first place.

He wiped the back of his hand over his forehead. But if the baby was his, she surely would have told him. At this point what was there to lose?

Unless she didn't trust him. Unless she was waiting until he committed to her.

He was suddenly feeling sick. When the waitress brought their food he asked for a glass of water.

"Are you okay?"

"I'm fine," he said sipping the water. "Just faced with the reality of adulthood."

"Yeah, it usually comes in your thirties and totally messes things up."

He chuckled. He wasn't sure he could wait a week to pop the question now.

The next hour and a half was a whirlwind of chaos, as Christian liked to think of it. Every woman in his life had an opinion on what they thought Tori would like. He realized he should have only invited Sonia, but as they hadn't done much speaking since he'd broken up with Tori, and it hadn't gone well then, it would have been even more tense than the conversations going on around him.

Clara had spotted a nice band. Nothing fancy, but with a nice engraved design. "She's simple beauty."

His Aunt Simone was shaking her head. "No. Even simple beauty wants something that says *Look at me!*"

His mother was quietly seated just beyond all the women huddled around the case.

"You don't want to help me?" He touched her shoulder.

"Oh, I'm here for you. I can't think of anyone I'd want to join our family more than Tori."

"Then why are you over here and not in the midst of that?" He pointed to the women in his family arguing over if Tori was a two-karat or a one-karat or a band-of-gold girl.

Madeline Keller pointed her manicured finger to a ring in the glass and then looked up at her son and smiled. "This one reminded me of Tori."

It was simple and screamed elegant. It wasn't among the engagement rings, it was an anniversary band. It had three diamonds, which were also not extravagant in size.

"One for Sam. One for Ali. One for you."

He could feel his lip twitch and it meant she'd caused him to want to cry. It was the most perfect ring for her. And in his mind the third diamond would be for the baby. And at that moment it didn't matter the paternity of the baby. What mattered is he wanted all three of those children and Tori.

He hugged his mother and kissed her on the cheek. "Tori is lucky to have you."

"No. She's lucky to have you."

Chapter Twenty

Victoria had already cleared the dinner table before Christian had walked through the door.

"I didn't think you were coming," she said, as her voice quivered as she said it.

"Don't give up on me yet. I texted you and told you I was coming."

She nodded. She didn't like not trusting that he'd show up. "I know. You just haven't missed a meal with us in almost three weeks."

"I don't intend on missing another one at all." He walked up behind her at the sink and wrapped his arms around her waist. She noticed his hands rested on her stomach and tiny butterflies let go inside of her.

"I'm sorry I doubted you. I want this to work out this time."

Christian turned her around to face him. He was so handsome. The mix of Italian and Puerto Rican blood that ran through him gave him that dark, mysterious look. There were hints of him that looked like his father, but his mother's gentleness had always resonated from him. Victoria smiled when she thought of how handsome or beautiful their baby would be.

She'd had a long night thinking about him after he'd left wearing the T-shirt she'd long ago stolen from him when they were engaged and happy before the accident. Christian had gone through a lot of loss in the past year, as had she. He'd dealt with it differently and she'd not had the chance to. Her role had changed overnight. With every day that passed that he was part of their family, she realized that whatever had taken over inside of him, causing him to leave her as he had, that just wasn't him. This man, who gazed at her with eyes of nothing, but admiration and love, was the man whom she wanted to share her life with.

She'd made a doctor's appointment for the next afternoon. And she'd already asked Sonia to watch the kids so she and Christian could have a night together. The plan was to tell him about the baby and ask him to marry her. She was quite confident he'd planned on asking her too, but under the circumstances and the secrecy, she thought it best if she asked.

Those butterflies in her stomach ramped up in flight and she took a deep breath.

"I have some dinner left over," she offered as Chris's hand came to her cheek.

"I'll settle for dessert." He moved in and his mouth took hers. There was no softness, no ease into the moment. There was a heat that burned from his tongue to hers.

She gripped the front of his shirt and pulled him closer until there was no room between them.

"Wow. I sure have missed those kisses." Chris rested his forehead against hers.

"Me too."

"My mom wants me to invite you all over for dinner tomorrow."

Victoria bit down on her lip. "Can we take a rain check? I don't have to work, so I asked Sonia to watch the kids, so you and I could have a nice dinner. Just the two of us."

She could feel what the moment and suggestion was doing to him, but he was fighting the manly urges she knew rattled in his body.

"I'll tell her to wait. Maybe," he moved in again closer, "we can share some news with her when we do go over."

Victoria swallowed hard as Chris stepped away when the kids ran through the kitchen. Did he know? How could he know? Had Sonia or Scott...no. Scott wouldn't do that and Sonia wouldn't breach her trust. Maybe this was making him think about proposing. Should she do it now? Should she ask him and then tomorrow tell him about the baby? She had it in her head that having the picture would be the best way to do that. He wouldn't be able to get mad when he saw what they created.

Her hands began to shake.

Chris picked up both kids and they gave him hugs. Those butterflies in her stomach must have multiplied, because it caused her to run to the bathroom and release the dinner she'd just eaten.

She tried to kick at the door so it would shut, but Chris was right there.

"How long does this last?" He asked and her eyes opened wide.

"I'm sure it was just nerves."

"What could you possibly be nervous about?" He pulled the hand towel off the hook, wet it and handed it to her.

"Us. This. Your mom."

"My mom? What could make you nervous about her? She loves you."

"She does?"

He sat on the floor of the bathroom across from her. "You belong in my family. You know that. Sweetheart, I'm sorry for all the pain I caused you. I promise to make it up to you."

"I just hope you won't hate me."

His eyebrows narrowed. "I can't think of a reason in the world I would hate you."

She could and that had her throwing up again.

Christian drove away from the house close to midnight. He'd hoped to stay—to make love to Tori all night, but she was worked up about something and he could only assume that she was worked up over the baby.

Since she still hadn't told him about it, he had to only assume that the baby really was Scott's. But, Christian was a Keller and Kellers didn't let the opportunity to raise a baby born of someone else's blood go unloved. His father and his aunts were adopted. Darcy had been an adopted baby and her parents had loved her unconditionally. Having Ali and Sam as his family and this baby which Tori is carrying—well it just made sense to him.

He was taking that damn ring with him tomorrow and he was going to give it to her whether she was ready for it or not. And he was going to pack a suitcase and start moving in. He didn't want to leave the house at midnight anymore. He wanted to live there with her and the kids. This mistake he made couldn't dictate the rest of his life. It needed to be over. He needed to move forward and he was going to do that with his family.

~*~

Victoria lay on the table in the doctor's office. Her heart was racing as the doctor got the machine ready for them to look at her baby. Guilt was burning her gut. She should have invited Christian. She was about to hear the heartbeat of their baby. She was about to see their baby for the first time. Keeping this a secret wasn't fair to him. He was missing out on this very special moment.

But at that moment the doctor turned to her. "Are you ready?"

She nodded and he put the jelly on her stomach and then the wand to her skin.

He maneuvered it for a moment until, on the screen, came the small image of her baby.

The doctor turned on the volume and she heard the rapid heartbeat. Tears streamed from her eyes. This was the most precious and wonderful moment in her life.

"The baby looks good. We don't usually look this early, but sometimes moms can bat their eyes just right."

"You have no idea what this means to me. Thank you."

She let the tears continue to stream down her face. The doctor took measurements and made different angle pictures that were then filed digitally. At the end, he printed a picture which showed the baby's outline. Though it wasn't much more than a bubble it was hers and Chris's bubble. This was the most beautiful baby Victoria had ever seen.

"Here you go. A keepsake." He handed her the picture. "Do you have any questions?"

"When will I stop being sick?"

He patted her shoulder. "You should see that subside very soon. You're almost through your first trimester. Just take it easy."

She nodded and gazed back down at the picture in her hand as the doctor left the room. "Hello, baby." She ran her fingers over the image. "I love you so much."

~*~

Christian had taken the day off. The baseball field would manage one day without him. He had things to do.

Comments had been made by Tori the night before insinuating that she planned to get back home from running errands by about four. He planned to be in the house by three.

Knowing the kids would be at Sonia's, he decided to start his day there.

Sonia's expression when she opened the door wasn't necessarily one of excitement.

"Chris, what are you doing here?"

"I wanted to talk to the kids."

She narrowed her eyes on him. "Tori isn't here. I don't know…"

He stepped up until he was right inside the screen door she held open. "I love her, Sonia. I'm not going to hurt her again. I want to marry her. I bought her a ring. Now I want to tell the kids about it. I want to make sure they are okay with it."

Her eyes went moist and he knew he'd pulled the right strings. "It has been a long year hating you. You were always good for her."

"I was wrong to do what I did."

"You were hurting."

"Yeah, well it clouded my better judgment. I'm not going to let that happen again."

Sonia chewed on her lip. "You're sure you're okay with the kids and everything going on in her life?"

Christian played what she was saying over in his head. She didn't actually say anything about the baby, so he wouldn't either. "I'm ready for *anything.*"

Sonia stepped back and let him into the house.

When the kids saw him they ran to him, their arms open and then wrapped around him.

"Can I talk to you two?"

They each took one of his hands and they walked out to the living room. Christian sat the kids on the couch and knelt down in front of them.

"I want to ask you two a question. First of all, I want to tell you that your daddy was my very best friend. And when you were born, he asked me to take care of you. And I want to do that. I also want you to know I love your Aunt Tori."

Sam look unenthused, but there was a giant smile on Ali's mouth.

"I want to ask her to marry me and then we would all be a family—forever."

Ali clapped her hands together and Sam watched. Then he clapped his hands together.

"I want to know if you two would be okay with that?"

"Yes!" they both answered.

"And would it be okay if someday we had a baby or two? Would you be okay if more babies lived in our house?"

"Can I hold them?" Ali said enthusiastically.

"Of course. Someday, okay?"

She nodded.

"Okay. Now I want to show you something." He pulled the ring from his pocket and showed it to them. "I want to give this to Aunt Tori. Do you think she'll like it?"

"Yes. I like it! She will like it. Can I have one?"

He laughed and he could hear Sonia, just beyond the wall, laugh too.

"You want a ring? I'll buy you a ring. What about you, Sam? What do you want?"

"Baseball!"

Oh, this one was a kid after his own heart.

"Okay then." He pulled them into his arms and kissed each of them on the cheek. "You two stay with Sonia this evening and I'll give her the ring and see if she'll marry me."

As he left the house he wondered if he should have taken them with him. He still wasn't sure Tori was going to want to spend her life with him. He had a lot of making up to do for the year he'd let her take on the world alone.

Chapter Twenty-One

Christian arrived before she had. There were flowers on the table. Two champagne glasses next to the flowers and a bottle of sparkling cider, ready for celebration. Next to the glasses he'd displayed the ring.

If they made it to dinner then he would call in a favor at the restaurant a buddy owned.

It was nearing four o'clock. He looked at his watch nearly every minute, but she hadn't walked in the door yet and he was growing more nervous by the moment.

He was taken by surprise when the doorbell rang. He walked through the house and pulled open the door.

Scott stood on the front porch with a bouquet of flowers in his hands. He was dressed in a fancy suit and his expensive sunglasses begged to be broken into a million pieces.

"Oh, hi," he said as if he were surprised to find Christian standing in the doorway. "I didn't realize you'd be here. I wanted to talk to Victoria."

Christian bit down hard. "Tori isn't here. Why would you want to talk to her? I think the statutes of limitations on the apology you owe her has passed." He would have kept his tone kinder, but he couldn't find it in him to do so.

"I beg your pardon? What about you? What about the way you left her to deal with everything she had to deal with? You think she's got a better situation with you?"

Christian moved toward the man who had him by at least three inches in height and a solid build. But he'd push him into the street if he had to.

"Scott!" Victoria's voice came from the steps behind Scott. "What are you doing here?"

"I came to apologize for my behavior a few weeks ago. I was a bit stressed with work and wasn't prepared for what you'd told me."

Tori's eyes widened and she shot a glance to Chris. His gut twisted. Scott did know. She had told him about the baby and she'd left him out of the loop completely when it came to knowing.

"Scott, this isn't the very best time."

Christian stepped out of the house and stood facing both of them. "C'mon, Tori, let him apologize for his attitude. Let him apologize for walking out on you when you needed him."

"Chris," she said through gritted teeth. "You don't know what you're talking about."

He kept his glare on Scott. "Don't I? Don't I know that the moment you told him you were pregnant he walked out on you?"

He heard her gasp and Scott stepped up to him until their noses nearly touched.

"Well at least I see by your being here you stepped up to be a man. Though having a one night stand with someone else's girlfriend isn't what I'd consider being a man at all. But at least you're here, which leads me to believe you've taken your responsibilities seriously."

"Oh, Scott! Chris!" They both turned their eyes to Tori standing next to them. "Please, Scott, you have to go. Please."

"Fine. I thought you might have thought this through. I was willing to give your baby a name. Obviously his father has some anger issues."

His words were a blow to his already twisted gut. "What did you say?"

"You heard me." Scott dropped the flowers and moved in again so that he was face to face. "You sleep with someone's girlfriend and get her pregnant and I'm the one making an ass of myself? I don't know who you think you are, Mr. Keller, but this isn't the way to do things. If you were a real man…"

"Wait!" He held up his hand and then turned to Tori. "I got you pregnant?"

"Christ, man. She's not the kind of woman who just sleeps around. Give her some credit."

He was about to give Scott a fist to the jaw.

"Chris, let's go inside and talk."

"All this time I thought you were having his baby and it was mine?"

"Chris…"

"You didn't think you could tell me?"

Scott shook his head. "Right, because you might just walk out like you did when her sister died."

That was the last straw. Chris pulled his fist back to swing at the man, but found himself knocked on his ass.

"Oh, God!" Tori rushed to him. "Scott, what are you doing?"

"I'm walking away. I shouldn't have come in the first place." He looked at Christian. "For your information, asshole, I never even slept with her. And if you'd been the man in her life I wouldn't have even been involved. I came to take on your responsibility, because she's a good woman and the kids are fantastic kids."

Scott turned and walked down the steps and a moment later he was speeding off down the street.

Christian moved his jaw from side to side.

"If the baby was mine why didn't you tell me?"

She was sobbing now and that hurt him as much as his jaw.

"How did you know? I didn't tell you. I didn't tell anyone but Sonia."

"Well, he seemed to know."

She sat back on the ground. "He found the test. Chris, I didn't plan this. I just figured I'd raise the baby alone. You couldn't commit to a life with me and Scott walked away."

"You would have considered him over me? You would have let him raise my baby?"

There was some clarity for him.

He got to his feet. "Let's get this out in the open." He looked down at her not even offering her a hand. His attitude had changed from one of acceptance to blinding anger. "You are pregnant from our one night?"

She nodded and wiped the tears from her cheeks.

"And you didn't think it was important to tell me this in light of all the time we've been spending together?"

"I thought you'd be mad."

"I'm mad, because all this time I thought it was Scott's baby you were carrying and you were afraid I'd turn you away."

"I never slept with Scott."

"That's what makes this worse. Don't you see it? You don't even trust me enough to tell me that you're carrying my baby. *My* baby."

He reached into his pocket and pulled out his keys.

"Where are you going?" Tori struggled to stand. "Chris, what are you doing?"

"I need some time to think this though. If you can't trust me to be part of my own child's life, how can you trust me with anything?"

He saw her struggling, but he had to keep moving. Accepting the baby was one thing, but to know she held the information from him on purpose, that was what hurt. If she loved him like she said she did then she should have told him.

He put the keys in the ignition and started the truck. As she made it down the stairs he drove away.

Victoria stopped as the truck screeched around the corner. The tears fell freely now and her heart ached so that she thought she could die.

He was right. She hadn't told Christian about the baby because she couldn't trust him to stay.

She placed her hands on her stomach and held the tiny swell. Dear God, what had she done?

Dragging herself back toward the house she picked up her bag and walked inside.

She felt sick again. Her entire body shook and the tears wouldn't stop. Falling onto the couch, she let the sorrow of the moment take over and the tears rolled until she no longer had tears to cry.

By then, it was dark outside and she'd been on the couch for nearly three hours trying to put all the pieces of the past few months into place.

Finally, she stood and walked toward the kitchen. She'd long forgotten that in her car were groceries to make dinner for Chris. She was going to ask him to marry her and to have their baby. His reaction wasn't the one she'd wanted, but there was a part of her that had been prepared for it.

She thought about the picture that she had to show him. What would he think if he could see their baby? As she turned around to find the bag she'd drug in with her she noticed the flowers, the glasses, the sparkling cider—and the ring.

Her knees went weak and she grabbed hold of the back of the chair. What had she done?

It took her another hour to pull herself together. Once she did, she drove to Sonia's house where when Sonia opened the door she fell into her arms and cried even more.

"I should have told him. I should have told him right away," she sobbed against her best friend's shoulder. "He hates me. He left."

Sonia ran her hand over her hair. "Sweetheart, calm down."

"I can't. He's gone. I ruined it."

"No. Shhh." She kissed the top of her head. "Listen, give him some time."

"I can't. I messed it all up." Victoria sniffed. "I—I lied to him."

"You just didn't come forward when you should have."

"You *do* think I'm wrong."

"I think you're misjudging him. That's all." She wrapped her arm around Victoria's shoulders and walked her to the couch. She guided her down and sat next to her.

"Tell me what happened when you got home."

Victoria took some deep breaths and tried to get her composure. When she could she explained how everything happened when she got home. How Scott was there to apologize and how he told Christian all about the baby.

She long ago should have run out of tears, but she hadn't yet.

Then she told her about him leaving and how she then found the ring.

"A three diamond anniversary band?"

Victoria's eyes opened wide.

"Yes."

"He came here and asked the kids if he could ask you to marry him."

"Are you kidding me?" The tears were drying.

She shook her head. "He showed them the ring and Ali asked for one too."

That finally made her chuckle.

"What did he say to that?"

"That he'd buy her a ring and Sam wanted a baseball."

God he was wonderful and she'd let him out of her life a year ago without a fight and again when he drove away.

"What am I going to do?"

"Don't you suppose that he needs some time too?" She rubbed Victoria's back. "And when he was talking to the kids he asked them if it would be okay if the two of you had more kids. Do you think he knew?"

Victoria looked at her friend. "He did know." She shook her head as if she'd only just realized it. "He said he thought I was having Scott's baby." She wiped away the last of her tears. "He didn't say how he knew, but he knew."

She looked at Sonia who shook her head. "I didn't say a word."

"Last night when I got sick he asked how much longer it was supposed to last. He meant the morning sickness." She sucked in her breath. "Why didn't he tell me he knew? He just kept asking me if I had something to tell him."

"Calm down." Sonia took her hands in hers. "You need to just calm down. If he knew about the baby and even thought the baby belonged to another man *and* was still going to ask you to marry him, don't you suppose once he's done being angry that you didn't tell him he'll come back around? Tori, he loves you."

"I'm scared. I'm so scared."

Sonia pulled her back into her arms. "He's a Keller man. And Keller men don't let the women they love out of their grasp."

Victoria nodded at that. "I love him. I don't want to do this without him."

"Give him a few days."

She agreed, but she wasn't sure she'd survive a few days without him—not anymore.

Chapter Twenty-Two

The night was extremely dark. Christian sat on the tailgate of his pickup and looked out over the ball field which was still just piles of dirt.

Just like the field, where he could imagine the bleachers, the bases, the people cheering—he could imagine his life with Tori, the kids, and their baby.

He ran his fingers through his hair. Arianna had prepared him for the thought that the baby might be his, but he'd never really bought into that. It just didn't make sense, that if the baby was his, why didn't she tell him? And as angry as he was, what did it really matter? He loved her and Ali and Sam. And there was a part of him that loved that baby more than anything.

He let out a steady breath. He was going to be someone's father. Not their uncle or cousin or brother—their father.

His head began to spin as though he'd actually drank the bottle of Jack he'd bought, but the seal was still intact—he'd known better.

And then the thought in his head went full circle. He'd gone to her house that night when he'd found out she was pregnant, but it wasn't the reason. The reason he went back was because he loved her. The pregnancy was just a reason to get her to let him in. With or without the baby he'd always loved her. Nothing was going to take that away.

There'd been a little ring at the store that he'd remembered seeing. That ring belonged to Ali, he'd stop and pick it up. Sam needed a new baseball and Christian had the very one. He'd kept it for years—it was signed by his father.

He'd looked into coaching T-ball and maybe that would make the day of the young boy who was probably lost in all the talk about marriage and babies.

And of course the baby—oh he knew the perfect thing to buy the baby. He hoped Victoria would appreciate it too.

He'd go to her tomorrow as he did every night after work—and he wouldn't go back home. Never again.

~*~

When Christian walked into his brother's office the next morning he didn't look amused when Christian told him he needed another afternoon off.

"It's all for a good cause and everything is up to date," he promised.

"First you mope around all year and now you're gone all the time. What gives?"

Christian sat down in the chair in front of his brother's desk. "Well, I have to go buy a ring."

"Mom and Darcy said you did that already."

"Oh, I bought one for Tori. Now I have to buy one for Ali." Ed's look of confusion was priceless. "I just signed on to coach T-ball too."

"You did not."

"I did."

Ed laughed. "I think this is your calling."

"Well it looks like I have a baby on the way so…"

Ed came out of his chair and was on his feet. "No. Really?"

"Your wedding was a lucky night."

"You're kidding. Really?"

Christian stood and met his brother. "Really. So I need to get over there with rings and gifts and get this all solidified. I want her to marry me before the baby gets here. This is how it should have always been."

"Go. Take tomorrow too. But then, damnit, you'd better not miss another day."

"I'll do my best."

He made his stops around town. The baseball was in his house, in the room he'd made a shrine to his successes. It was all worthless now. Nothing could compare to what was about to come. A trophy was plastic. A wife and a family—that was forever.

The ring was small and the stone was pink. The man assured him that they could resize it if it didn't fit Ali. He'd thought buying a ring for Tori—twice—was hard. This had been harder.

His final stop before heading home to his *family*, was to buy a baby outfit that looked like a baseball uniform. On the back he had printed KELLER 15 to match the jerseys he'd once worn.

Now it was time to make amends and become a family.

It was nearly four-thirty when he pulled up in front of the house, but the minivan wasn't parked in the driveway. That was even better. He would go inside and be waiting.

When he walked into the kitchen the flowers were still on the table where he'd arranged them with the sparkling cider and the glasses. Still there was the ring he'd planned to give her. But there was a new addition to the items.

Christian moistened his lips as he sat down in the chair. Next to the ring was a small framed picture. The frame said OUR BABY and inside was a sonogram picture of just a little bubble—his bubble.

He could feel tears well in his eyes. That made it all very real.

The front door opened and Christian's heart rate kicked up. It was time. She was there and she wasn't going to kick him out—not ever again.

When he looked up Sonia was walking toward him. Her eyes were dark and her cheeks flushed.

"I thought I'd find you here. Your brother said you'd taken the day off."

His heart raced faster now, but now with a pain that he couldn't quite explain.

"You went to my office?"

She nodded as she looked at the table. "I have the kids at home with Craig." She moved closer to him and he now could see that her eyes were red and moist. "Tori's at the hospital."

His uncomfortable heart rate became nearly so painful that he had to put his hand on his chest to ease the discomfort.

"Is she okay? Is everything okay?"

Sonia shook her head. "She'll be fine. They are just keeping an eye on her. But, Chris, she lost the baby."

He'd never in his life burst into tears, but at that moment he did. The pain of her words was so incredibly sharp, that he felt like he might die in that chair. He felt as he did when he couldn't get to Dave to save his life in the crash. Christian Keller was helpless.

Sonia moved to him and he pulled her into his arms.

"I can give you a ride."

"I can get there," he said into her hair as she held him tight.

"Your uncle left the clinic and went up to the hospital to be with her. He's there now."

Of course he was. There was always a Keller man ready to help someone who needed them. He'd been the only one not to take that path the first time.

"I'm going to go to her," he said pulling away.

"She loves you. She's very distraught about the baby and not telling you."

He wiped his eyes. "None of this matters. She's what matters and she is what always mattered." He picked up the picture on the table. "There will be other babies."

She gazed up at him and smiled. "What are you going to do?"

"Be there like I should have always been."

He kissed Sonia on the cheek, picked up the ring, and headed out the door to the hospital to help Tori mourn what was lost and prepare to move on.

Chapter Twenty-Three

Curtis Keller was waiting just outside the elevator when Christian stepped off. He was in blue scrubs and had at least a day's worth of beard growth.

"Is she okay? Tell me *she's* okay."

Curtis moved to him and placed his hands on his nephew's shoulders. "Tori will be fine. Miscarriages at this stage aren't uncommon. She can go home in a little while. We're just getting her some fluids, because she's very dehydrated and some pain meds."

Christian nodded. "What? How?"

His uncle dropped his hands. "She began to have bleeding and pain. When that happened, she had Sonia bring her into the clinic. It happens, Chris. You have to understand that, it just happens. She didn't do anything wrong. There just was a reason that this baby didn't make it full term. It doesn't mean it'll affect her having more babies."

Christian nodded again. "I just want to see her."

"C'mon."

He walked him down the hall to a room where the door was open just slightly. He could hear her sobbing and that pained him.

"She's going to be okay," his uncle said, resting his hand on his shoulder again. "Just let her know you're here."

"Forever."

His uncle gave him a smile and walked away leaving him to be with her and heal her emotionally after having caused her so much grief.

Reaching for the door had been one of the hardest things he'd ever done. Walking away from things like this had always been easier and too often the road he'd taken.

Her back was turned to him when he walked in and shut the door, but she didn't turn to look.

"Tori." His voice was unsteady as he called to her.

She rolled toward him. Her eyes were swollen from all the tears she'd cried and her cheeks were wet. An IV line was taped to her wrist.

"You can go. You don't have to be here," she said on a sob.

"I'm not going anywhere."

"I'm not pregnant anymore. You don't have any responsibilities to me."

Christian swallowed hard. He could argue with her, but he wasn't going to. This was the moment he needed to know what it was to be a man and accept life in all of its ugliest forms.

He moved to the edge of the bed and looked down at her. Her blonde hair was matted to the side of her face and her skin was red from all the crying.

Without invitation he sat at the edge of the bed. "I'm heartbroken over the baby."

"So am I," she said softly.

"I saw the picture on the table."

That seemed to upset her as the tears came harder. "Just-yesterday," she sobbed. "How-can it go-so bad?"

"Curtis said this just happens, but doesn't mean it'll happen with your next pregnancy."

She shook her head. "I won't do this again. No."

Christian reached up and placed his hand on her cheek. "We will."

"We? You think you're going to keep me after this? After I didn't trust you? After I didn't tell you?"

"Tori, I'm never going anywhere. Don't you understand? I love you. I've been a lousy fiancée this year. But the vows are through sickness and health until death do us part. Well, all of that got thrown at us in one year. And I didn't handle it well."

"Right. So why are you here?"

"Like I said, I love you."

He scooted up further on the bed and Tori adjusted until he was lying next to her, facing her, and holding her hand.

"Does this hurt you?" he asked as he rested his hand on her hip.

"No."

"Good." With his other hand he brushed back her hair and then rested his head on his hand and looked down at her. "I did this all wrong. You paid for it."

Her tears seemed to be drying. That, he thought, was a good sign.

"Tori, I don't want to live my life without you or Ali or Sam. I love those kids. And I love you. This year taught me something. I'm very selfish and I'm horrible at facing things I don't want to face."

She chuckled and she wiped away her tears. "I never pegged you to be that guy."

"Me either. Though Ed was always the stronger one. I remember when mom had cancer and dad shaved her head." He smiled at the memory. "When they were done, dad stepped in and told her to shave his head. And then Ed did the same."

The vision was as clear in his mind as the day it had happened. "I'll never forget Dad looking at me and Clara in the bathroom door asking us which one was next."

He looked back at her. "I ran away that day too. I was never good at this."

"You've done okay the past few weeks."

"Yeah, well I would like to keep trying. I'm going to stumble and I'm going to fall—a lot."

"I missed you when you weren't with me," she said softly the tears now dry. "It was as if a part of me had been torn away with my sister."

"I know."

"And this baby—it was my chance to have that part of you I was always supposed to have."

"We'll have that again," he promised her as he rubbed her exposed arm. "Will you keep me?"

"I come with a lot of baggage."

"Yeah, well I like your baggage. I'm a T-ball coach now, you know?"

She smiled wide. "You are?"

He nodded. "Some great kid wants to be a ball player like his dad."

Her eyes began to moisten again, but the tears weren't sad. "He is a great kid."

Christian reached into his shirt pocket and pulled out the little ring he'd bought for Ali. "There's a sweet little girl who said I could marry you too if I bought her a ring."

Those happy tears began to fall. "You bought her a ring?"

"Looks like something she'd love, doesn't it?"

Tori nodded and then looked up at him. "I saw the ring on the table."

"Yeah, I was setting up a romantic night that you'd find it hard to turn down a marriage proposal."

Her body began to shake and Christian pulled the blanket up over her. IVs always made him cold too.

She licked her lips. "I was going to propose to you," she said looking up at him through tear soaked lashes.

"Me?" He pulled back and looked at her. "Why?"

Tori chuckled. "I wanted to have our baby together and I thought if I asked you then you'd know you were wanted."

"I knew I was wanted when I came to your house and you were wearing my clothes."

"They are my favorite."

"You can have them. I brought a suitcase of others with me. It's just the first load. I'll bring the rest of my stuff over the next few weeks."

Tori reached up and touched his cheek, the IV line following. "You're going to move in with us?"

"We're a family right?"

She nodded. "I think we are."

"Well, I'll move in, but you have to do me a favor."

"What's that?"

"When they pull all this crap off of you, you have to wear this." He reached into his pocket again and pulled out the ring he'd picked out for her.

"Oh, Chris."

"My mother picked it out. One stone for Ali, one for Sam, and she said the other was for me, but I figured it was for the baby."

Her tears came back and he brushed them away.

"Don't be sad. That baby will always be our first and he or she will be waiting for us on the other side."

That seemed to resonate with her and she nodded as she wiped away the new tears.

Chris handed her the ring and she looked at it and then back at him.

"Be my wife. Take my name. Let me be there to raise Ali and Sam and keep the spirit of their parents alive. Have another baby with me. And another, and another…"

"Okay. Okay," she laughed as she took the ring and fisted it in her hand.

"T-ball coach, really?"

"Yeah. I just landed the biggest home run ever, now it's time to teach that little man how to hit one too."

Epilogue

There was a pep-band in the stands and twenty suited T-ball players on the field. It had taken some arm twisting, but Christian had somehow worked his charm so that the first game played in the new stadium was his team.

Sam had on his jersey which read HORTON 3, in honor of his father.

Ali had convinced Avery to buy her a cotton candy and she sat next to Victoria, who waved. Her wedding ring sparkled in the sunlight.

The sight had Christian looking down at his own hand at the gold band on his finger. He never thought a piece of jewelry could say so much.

No other babies had come along yet, but that' hadn't stopped the newlyweds from trying their hardest.

Christian placed the helmet on Sam's head and gave it a tap on the top.

"You got this?"

Sam, who had just turned four, winked. "I got this."

"Hit it out of the park kid."

Sam took his bat and walked up to the tee. Christian watched as he eyeballed each base and then looked to the outfield. It's a move Christian had seen Sam's father do, and mimicking Babe Ruth, he pointed to the outfield.

With all his might Sam took the bat back behind his shoulder and gave it a mighty swing. The bat hit the whiffle ball off the tee and it flew through the air—out to the field where he'd pointed.

Christian's heart began to race and he could hear Tori and Ali and the rest of his family shouting Sam's name as he passed by first base, and second base, and third base, and all the way home where Christian was there with his arms wide open to catch him as he scored his very first home run.

5 Prince Publishing and Bernadette Marie hope you've enjoyed

Home Run

*Please enjoy the first chapter of the upcoming 8th book in
the Keller Family Series*

The Acceptance
Coming May 2014

Chapter One

There was something about an airport. People were coming and going. Some were heading out for adventure and some were heading home—just like Tyler Benson.

Nashville would always be home. He'd taken nearly three years to see the world and think his life through. He wasn't sure he had a better grasp on it yet, but he knew one thing—he missed his family.

Why had he let his mother's choices affect him so much? Things must have been pretty bad for her if she gave up a child and never spoke of it again.

The man in him understood. She was protecting him and his brother from what had happened to her when she'd fallen in love with an abusive man who tried to kill her. But the boy in him was still hurt.

Heading back wouldn't fix everything. He assumed there'd be a lot of late night talks over the kitchen table as there had been when he was a teenager. His father had already offered him a good job in the construction firm which had been in the family for generations. And—he needed to finally get to really know his sister.

Darcy had been as shocked as Tyler when she'd learned who her mother was. After all, she'd fallen in love with Tyler's cousin—that had to have been a little odd. But the Keller family was eclectic. It was made up of lots of adopted children, but they were still one big family.

His cousin Ed and his sister Darcy had been married over a year now. Their wedding had been the only time Tyler had been home in three years. Now it was time to face his parents and ask for some forgiveness, though he was sure they'd give it to him. Everyone understood his need to find himself.

They called his flight from New York to Nashville and it was time to board the plane. He stood and moved toward the line as a woman ran right into him.

"I'm so sorry," she said quickly.

"It's no problem." He looked down and noticed she'd dropped her scarf. "You dropped this." He bent down to pick it up and hand it to her.

The woman only held out her hand, but didn't reach for it. Tyler placed it in her open hand.

"Oh, thank you. I lose more things." She gave a casual laugh and continued on. It was then he noticed the cane in her other hand.

"Do you need an arm to get on the plane?"

She smiled at him, though her eyes were shielded behind big sunglasses. "Are you a nice man or do you feel sorry for me?"

That was quite a question, he thought. "Well, I'd like to think it was because I was raised right."

"You're from the South." She thought a moment. "Tennessee?"

"Yes. Born and raised in Nashville."

She leaned in closer to him. "I guessed from your accent and since we're getting on a flight bound that way."

He couldn't help but chuckle. "Offer still holds."

"What's your name?"

"I'm Tyler. Tyler Benson."

"Courtney Fields and, Mr. Benson, I'd love to have you guide me if you don't mind."

"It would be my pleasure."

He let her take his arm, though she didn't interlock elbows, instead she held the back of his arm just above his elbow.

When they approached the door Courtney held out her ticket and the woman scanned the ticket and placed the stub back in her hand. She then did the same for Tyler.

Once checked in, they walked down the jet bridge.

"Do you travel a lot, Mr. Benson?"

"It's Tyler, and I've been doing my fair share the past few years. How about you?"

"I've been seeing the world, though not intentionally. So yes. I travel quite a bit. But this is a special trip back home."

He desperately wanted to ask her why she said she'd been seeing the world. Could she see? Was it just a figure of speech?

"Hello, Ms. Fields." The stewardess greeted her as they walked on board.

"Celia." Courtney smiled having obviously recognized the woman's voice. "I didn't expect you on this flight."

"I'm state side now." Celia took Courtney's hand which still held her cane and patted it. "I've heard we have your brother on board," she said softly.

Courtney nodded. "Finally."

"Your family has been in my thoughts for a long time."

"Thank you," Courtney said. "Oh, Celia, this is Tyler. My arm candy for the walk down the jet way."

Celia looked at Tyler and then back at Courtney. "I thought you had an escort."

"It's always good to make a new friend. How's he look?"

Celia scanned another look over him. "You did good."

Tyler forced a smile. "Thank you?"

Celia laughed. "Courtney, can I help you find your seat?"

"If you don't mind, I'll use my arm candy."

Tyler looked at her ticket. "You're in 3A."

"Yep, that sounds right. Where are you?"

"I'm in 4F."

"You like the window too?"

"Luck of the draw really."

Courtney stopped and turned back to Celia. "Can you see if you can arrange my escort to trade to 4F?"

The smile on Celia's face and the look she casually gave to Tyler made him a little nervous. His good deed had warranted him a seat change?

"Do you mind sitting by me on the flight? I could use some good company."

Tyler thought about the past three years and wondered if he could be good company. But, like he'd told her before, he'd been raised right. And if the woman wanted to sit by him, who was he to turn her down?

"If the other passenger doesn't mind changing I'd be happy to switch."

"I still like the window. I hope that's okay," she said as she walked toward her seat.

Once they were seated Courtney turned to him. "Thank you for picking up my scarf."

"You're welcome."

"Thanks for keeping me company. This trip home is a hard one and it'll be nice to have a handsome man to talk to."

He wondered what made her trip so hard, besides the obvious hindrance of not being able to see the world around her.

"How do you know I'm so handsome? Celia might have been lying to you."

She smiled. "Oh, I can tell you're handsome. And you're not married. I would guess you're in your mid to late twenties. You were well educated. You're about six-two. And I'm going to guess that you have blue eyes."

He knew that staring at her with his eyes wide open wasn't going to make her aware of how stunned he was, but for some reason he was sure she knew.

"How do you know all that?"

The smile on her mouth turned into a playful pucker forcing her cheeks to dimple on both sides. "You handed me my scarf with your left hand. You don't have a ring."

"You felt for a ring?"

"I dropped the scarf on purpose. You smelled good."

That made him laugh aloud. "Okay, keep going."

"I've held the arms of many people. I'm five-five, so I know my heights from there."

"I'm six-three."

"I was close."

"My education?"

"You have an accent, but your words have a refined quality to them. I'd guess you can speak more than one language."

"My father speaks French, and so does my aunt. I've always known both."

She nodded slowly as though she were collecting her reward for knowing so much.

"Okay, those are all logical. How do you know I have blue eyes?"

"That one was a guess, but I was right. You just told me."

"You have quite a talent."

Courtney turned her head toward the window. "You also seemed lost."

"I beg your pardon. How would you know that?"

"I could feel it. It felt as though you could use some company and I sure know I could."

He wasn't sure how this woman could tell so much about him, but she had a keen sense of the world around her.

The last passenger to board the plane was a soldier in uniform. As he passed by their row, he looked down at Courtney as if he knew she'd be there and then he continued to his seat which Tyler noted was the seat he was to have occupied.

As the doors were secured, the pilot came over the speaker.

"Ladies and Gentlemen, we will be starting our flight shortly. I wanted to inform you that we have the honor of flying home a vet to his final resting place today."

The air in the plane grew thick and Tyler could hear the many gasps and even sobs which had come from that announcement. He turned toward Courtney who had gripped her hands in front of her and pressed her forehead to her white knuckles.

"Are you okay?"

She lifted her head and he could see the tears streak down her cheek from under her sunglasses. Hesitantly she nodded.

"I'm finally getting to make the journey to take my brother home."

Tyler let out a long breath and watched as this woman he'd just met turned her face toward the warmth of the sun coming in through the small window.

He'd gained a sister and felt like his world had ended.

Courtney had lost a brother and yet was thankful to be with him on his final ride home.

Tyler rested his head against the back of his seat. His life didn't make any more sense than it had three years ago when he'd left Nashville. But at least when he got there his brother, sister, and his parents would be there.

What was there for Courtney?

Meet the Author

Damon Kappel ©2009

Bestselling Author Bernadette Marie is known for building families readers want to be part of. Her series *The Keller Family* has graced bestseller charts since its release in 2011, along with her other series and single title books. The married mother of five sons promises *Happily Ever After always*...and says she can write it, because she lives it.

When not writing, Bernadette Marie is shuffling her sons to their many events—mostly hockey—and enjoying the beautiful views of the Colorado Rocky Mountains from her front step. She is also an accomplished martial artist with a second degree black belt in Tang Soo Do.

A chronic entrepreneur, Bernadette Marie opened her own publishing house in 2011, *5 Prince Publishing*, so that she could publish the books she liked to write and help make the dreams of other aspiring authors come true too.

Visit Bernadette Marie at www.bernadettemarie.com

CPSIA information can be obtained at www.ICGtesting.com
Printed in the USA
LVOW07s2001260814

401025LV00001B/43/P